"Are you running away?"

The words came as if from a distance. Josh tore his gaze from the blue flames and stared into her big brown eyes. "Excuse me?"

She propped a hand on her hip and moved so she could look directly at him. "You can't bear to see your parents fighting, so you're running away."

He placed his palm on her cheek and ran his thumb along her chin. "Always thinking. I don't want to talk about the past and I don't want to talk about the future. Why don't we just stay in the moment, Miss Valentine?" And with that he pulled her into his arms and kissed her.

Thanksgiving night, a fire in the fireplace, together with a woman he liked and respected. This was all he wanted for now. Because once Miss Wendy Valentine found out the truth about him, there would be no more kisses. Once Miss Wendy Valentine found out what he'd done, she would have her big story and she would be on her way.

Dear Reader,

You're reading my second book! For whatever reason this book ended up in your hands, I thank you for reading this story. I strive to improve with each work, to write a story impossible to put down and to keep you reading long into the night. Thank you for the positive words and encouragement on this writing journey. Again I thank the crew at Harlequin, without whom this story would not be told. Again I am honored to be part of the Harlequin Heartwarming group of authors.

In *An Allegheny Homecoming*, Wendy and Josh leave the foothills of the Alleghenies. Josh because he's hiding a secret and Wendy because she seeks an opportunity she can't find in a small town. This exodus happens every day in small towns across the country. Whether one joins the military, seizes a job opportunity, or just craves adventure and new horizons, the urge to travel and explore is common to everyone.

But sometimes you just need to come home, to a place as familiar and comfortable as an old sweatshirt from your high school days.

Return to Bear Meadows with Josh Hunter.

As always...enjoy the read.

T.R.

HEARTWARMING

An Allegheny Homecoming

—

T. R. McClure

⊞ HARLEQUIN® HEARTWARMING™

Recycling programs
for this product may
not exist in your area.

ISBN-13: 978-0-373-36837-2

An Allegheny Homecoming

Copyright © 2017 by Tanya R. Schleiden

Printed in U.S.A.

T. R. McClure wrote her first story when she was ten years old. A degree in psychology led to a career in human resources. Only after retirement did she pick up her pen and return to fiction.

T.R. lives in central Pennsylvania with her husband of thirty-seven years. They share their country home with one horse, one cat, four beagles and Sunny the yellow Lab. T.R. is always up for travel adventures with her grown twin daughters.

Books by T. R. McClure

Harlequin Heartwarming

Wanted: The Perfect Mom

To my parents, Clyde and Stephania,
who gave me a loving and supportive family
environment but left this earth much too soon.

And to my husband's parents,
Elmer and Mary,
who gave me the opportunity to be
a daughter again.

CHAPTER ONE

"A COLD FRONT coming in from the north gives our area a dusting of snow for the overnight forecast." Wendy Valentine turned toward the camera with a smile. "So far this week it's been mild, but then into the weekend it becomes colder." Eyes on the monitor, she waved a hand over the center of the green screen. "Tuesday we'll have 44 degrees with a few passing clouds. High Wednesday only 37 with a few snow showers Thursday morning."

From his position behind the anchor desk, Casey Knight flashed bright, white teeth in her direction. His thick blond hair gleamed under the lights. "Thanks, Wendy, what a nice way to start the week, with a few more warm days before winter sets in. Not bad for central Pennsylvania in November."

"But don't forget it looks like snow

later in the week!" Elbows tucked, Wendy linked her fingers and rested her hands at her waist as the camera pulled back. "Better dig out your snow boots, Casey."

"This will be my first experience with snow since I moved here. I'm not sure I'm ready." With a charming grin and a sly wink, Casey spoke to camera one. "Well, that does it for us this morning. Stay tuned for national news. Our chief meteorologist, Mark Murphy, and I will see you at noon."

Wendy bit the corner of her lip to stop her frowning as she gazed at the new anchor. This was who she had lost the position to? This Mr. Perfect? Navy blazer, crisp white shirt, blue-and-gray-striped tie. No one should look that good, even if he was the new morning anchor for WSHF. "And we're clear." The voice of their college intern came out in a high-pitched squeak.

Wendy hadn't taken two steps before Casey was at her side. "Join me for a cup of coffee, Wendy? We should get to know each other." He winked.

"I'm going home. But maybe another time."

Casey looked her up and down. "You have a nice camera presence. You should try for an anchor position sometime. Catch ya later." Another wink and he was gone.

Wendy shrugged off the comment and her blazer just as a bead of sweat rolled down the side of her face. No matter how cold her forecast, under these lights the temperature was usually hot. Yet she always wore a suit in an attempt to be taken seriously by her peers. So far it hadn't worked.

She weaved through the collection of television equipment and thick cables strung across the floor to get to the hallway, en route to the tiny office she shared with the chief meteorologist. With more seniority than she, Mark had the cushy working hours of noon and six, leaving Wendy with early morning and late evening. The man wouldn't show at the station until shortly before the noon report. On the plus side, Wendy had all day to search for that one perfect story that would shoot her to the top and far away from this small-town television station.

"Wendy, could I see you for a minute?"

Another new addition to the station, Walt Crosby stuck his head into the hallway. The station manager's thick white hair appeared perpetually tousled. Red blotches colored his cheeks. Rumors of an incident on the West Coast that chased him east had accompanied his recent arrival.

On her way to the coffee station for her first cup, Wendy resisted the urge to frown. She couldn't afford to antagonize the man. Part of her plan involved doing something, anything, other than weather, and she needed his approval. "Sure, boss." She made a U-turn and followed Walt into a cluttered office, which no longer smelled of the former station manager's perfume but of smoke. "What's up?"

The husky man lifted a pile of newspapers from the single chair in front of his desk and motioned for her to sit. He settled into his own chair with a heavy sigh. Rolled-up shirtsleeves displayed hairy, muscular forearms. "We haven't had a chance to talk yet. Did you know Mark will be gone for the next three days?" He didn't sound pleased with the chief meteorologist.

Wendy was curious. "He is? Since when?"

"Since he had Sharon approve it before he left. Apparently the man has an uncanny knack for predicting snowfall. He's headed to Vermont to ski."

Wendy slumped in her chair. She knew what that meant. She would be doing the early morning, noon, evening and eleven o'clock weather. In other words, she would be living at the station. She hadn't complained when Mark had married last year and spent a month in Cancun for his honeymoon. But skiing? "So I've got it all."

"You have a problem with that?" At the end of the sentence, his bushy eyebrows rose, almost meeting in the middle.

Wendy bristled at the man's tone. She kept her answer short. "I can handle it." She had seen Mark just last Friday. Funny the man hadn't bothered to mention he had planned to take a few weekdays off, but then, ever since the news of her Atlanta offer had made the rounds at the station he had distanced himself.

The wooden desk chair creaked in protest as Walt leaned back and cupped his hands behind his head, as if trying to figure out if she were telling him the truth. "He already had the leave approved by the time I arrived. Sharon must have thought you could do it."

"To be honest, the three years I've been here Mark has always taken off for fresh powder. Early this year, though." Wendy drummed her fingers on the arm of her wooden chair. Her chair didn't tilt back.

Walt stared at the tile ceiling. Then he stretched and brought his chair forward with a thump. "The station had additional staff then."

Wendy nodded. "Budget cuts." She looked around the small office and wondered how much, if any, the previous station manager had shared with Walt. Sharon knew all about Wendy's drive to the big time. And she had almost made it. "How often did you talk with Sharon before she left?"

He pulled a cigar from his center desk drawer and stuck it in one corner of his mouth. "In the thirty seconds she had to tell me everything I needed to know, she might have mentioned you had an offer from an Atlanta affiliate last year." He held

her gaze. "I understand the job didn't materialize."

Wendy squirmed. "That's one way to put
it." She had been mortified, after telling
everyone and his brother she was leaving,
the deal had fallen through. Walt seemed
to be waiting for more. She was well aware
of the technique. Don't say anything, until
the person across from you felt compelled
to fill the silence and blurted out the information you're looking for. She never
seemed to have an opportunity to use it.
Lips pressed tightly together, she met the
gaze of the blue-eyed newsman sitting
across the messy desk.

Walt smiled. He rested muscular forearms on top of the papers strewed across
the desk. The cigar bounced up and down.
"And then the news anchor job came open,
and they brought in Casey from Georgia.
I'll bet that rattled you, eh?"

Wendy squirmed some more. If Sharon
hadn't told the man how hard she had lob-
bied for the position, then she was better
off if Walt never knew. "Casey has a great
on-air personality. I'm totally on board."
She had been so sure the anchor position

was hers. Casey's sparkling white teeth had won over the higher-ups and here she was, still doing the weather for WSHF in rural central Pennsylvania.

"Hmm. I'd wondered how you felt about the shake-up." Walt's mouth tilted in what Wendy assumed was a grin. "Did you ask your sister for advice?"

Shock ricocheted through her body. "What sister?"

"What sister?" Walt laughed out loud, a big booming laugh that seemed to ricochet around the small office. "How could I not know about your sister? She's famous in this business. Anchor on a national news desk at twenty-five, interviewer of the rich and famous for the last ten years. Not to mention you share the same last name." He tapped his forefinger on his head.

Wendy's heart thumped in her chest as she fought to calm her breathing. She and her sister looked nothing alike. Katie was tall and blond. Wendy was short and dark. Each took after her mother. "I want to make it on my own merit."

Walt nodded. "Sure you do. You majored in broadcasting, minored in journalism and took six credits in meteorology. And your first job is in your hometown. As a weather girl."

Wendy bit her tongue to keep from correcting the man. He was in the news business, and he still used the term *weather girl*? "This was the first offer I got. I didn't think I'd be here this long but, hey, the economy."

"The economy." He picked up a painted shot glass and held it with two fingers. "Which is why I expect you to stick with the weather. If I want interviews, I'll send Casey. Is that going to be a problem?"

The new station manager was giving her a warning. He didn't care if she wanted a different job or not. He had a station to look after. "Of course not." Wendy readjusted her position on the hard wooden chair. "Look, Walt, I have to run home and get back by noon. Was there anything else you wanted to discuss?" She didn't say she had hoped for a few minutes of respite at The Wildflower, the local coffee shop in Bear Meadows, where the baristas made the perfect nonfat vanilla latte.

Walt didn't seem to have heard her. He

continued to play with the shot glass for several seconds. "You live about twenty miles from here, right?"

She shouldn't have been surprised he knew where she lived. He was, after all, a newsman. "A few miles outside of Bear Meadows."

"You know how to operate the camera?" One bushy eyebrow raised as he finally set the shot glass next to the desk lamp and caught her gaze.

She nodded. "Absolutely." Part of her internship had been setting up the camera and then doing her own reporting without the help of a camera operator.

"Why don't you take one of the smaller cameras with you and do the weather from a remote location? Pick something picturesque. You can email the report in, and at least you'll be out of the studio." A flash of teeth again.

To avoid the sharp-eyed gaze, Wendy stared at the floor. Framed photographs filled a cardboard box. The one on top looked like Walt in front of... She squinted. *Mount Kilimanjaro?* What was he doing in little Shadow Falls? She wondered if the shot glass had anything to do with it. "Um, if you say so." Carting a piece of camera equipment around with her sounded like a pain; on the other hand, she wouldn't have to drive back to Shadow Falls for the noon report. She could go straight home. "Anyplace in particular you have in mind?"

Walt directed his attention to the television overhead, dismissing her. The low murmurings of the national news filled the silence. "You know this area better than I do. You decide."

Wendy's mind started spinning. She pictured the perfect spot. The bridge over Little Bear Creek. It was on the way home. And she would still have time for a latte. She deserved one, extra-large.

JOSH HUNTER FINISHED securing the fence that had been pressed to the ground by a fallen tree. The cattle had already been moved into the lower pastures for the winter, but there could be a few strays still wandering the high mountains of the northern Montana ranch. It was hard, but satisfying work. Although he still wasn't sure they actually needed a ranch hand here, or if his friend Matt hadn't convinced his uncle to find a job for Josh.

Four months out of the military and Josh still didn't know what he was doing next. But no matter. He had saved every penny of his army paycheck, so had enough money to get by for quite a while.

Giving a final pull to the fencing tool, he leaned back onto his heels and looked out over the plains. The mountains beyond were already covered with snow. He wondered if Bear Meadows had seen snow yet.

The last time he had gone home, over three years ago, his mother had made halupkis. Even now, thoughts of a roasting pan filled with the rolls of cabbage stuffed with hamburger and rice made his mouth water. She had cooked Easter dinner, like she always did. He thought everything had been fine. With his parents, that was.

But in his mind, every person he saw on the street seemed to know what he had done, albeit that was impossible. So he'd returned to base as soon as he could. Of course his guilty conscience probably had a lot to do with his paranoia.

A twig snapped, pulling him out of his

daydreaming. Still crouched by the fence, he half turned and caught a glimpse of tawny eyes peering at him from behind a fir tree.

Josh's breathing stilled. Pennsylvania born and raised, he had never been to Montana before. He knew all the critters in the eastern woods, but Montana was a different story. He reached for his rifle, then remembered he had left it in the truck, certain the wire fence would be a quick fix.

His knee dropped to the ground, the better to support the shift of his upper body. A big cat. A mountain lion. Rarely seen back east, but still plentiful in the west. The animal was beautiful. Long, sinewy body. A muted solid gold. The long tail brushed the ground.

"I'm just passing through, buddy." Josh's voice was low.

One tawny ear twitched. He couldn't seem to look away from the unblinking amber eyes.

"Take it easy, fella." Josh kept his breathing shallow, afraid of startling the animal. Being mauled by a mountain lion wouldn't be the worst way to go. His last vision would be of the endless Montana sky. *Yes, it could be worse.* "You're a beautiful animal. What do you want with me?"

The sound of hoofbeats reached his ears. The cat's ears pricked. Josh's gaze shifted right. When he looked back, the cat was gone.

"How you makin' out, buddy?" Matt MacDougal trotted up on the other side of the fence and reined in his horse. A compact man, he looked right at home on the big ranch horse. He lifted off his cowboy hat and ran a hand over short-cropped red hair.

Josh stood. His right knee cracked. "I just saw a mountain lion."

"No kidding? You have your rifle with you?"

"It's in the truck."

"Good place for it. You know a horse would've been able to carry you down that rocky slope, so you'd have your rifle handy. And Blue's in the barn getting fat. He could use some exercise."

"I told you the first day of boot camp I prefer my horses under the hood. Just because you can ride anything on four legs doesn't mean the rest of us can."

"If you say so, but the day is gonna come when the only way you can get somewhere is on one of these fellas. It's not that hard. You just sit here and let the horse do all the work." He ran a hand down the crown of the thick mane.

"You make it sound easy."

"Riding is easy." Matt grunted. "Aunt Steff wants you to come over to the main house for lasagna. She said *tell him no arguments*."

His stomach grumbled. He had been eating food out of a can for weeks. "I'll be there in a bit."

"That's what you said yesterday. You missed Sunday roast. You're gonna lose your social skills if you stay up here in this cabin much longer."

"What social skills?" Josh grinned and stared past his friend into the valley below. He could just make out the roof of the large barn.

"Got a point there, brother." He leaned on the saddle horn and looked up at the screech of a hawk. His sweat-stained Stetson dangled from his fingers. "You know, we should cut the rest of these dead trees before they fall."

Josh rubbed his right knee, which only bothered him when he put weight on it for extended periods of time. "I can do it."

"Why don't you wait until I can give you a hand? It's a two-man job." Matt fiddled with a rope hanging from the saddle horn. "You okay up here by yourself? You know, we have room at the house. Because there's no signal up here. If you need a hand…"

"Thanks, but I love it here in the mountains." Josh filled his lungs with a deep breath of the cool, crisp air and released it before answering. He gave his friend a confident stare. "I'll be fine."

"Well, you ever need to talk you know where to find me."

Josh met his gaze and nodded before glancing away. "Thanks." If he talked to anyone it would be to Matt, a man he trusted with his life. But Josh had managed to stay quiet for eight years; no sense dragging up the past at this late date.

Matt slapped his hat back on and tilted his head. "You know, you're starting to look like a crazy mountain man. You ever gonna shave? I can hardly recognize you." Matt's grin dissipated the tension in the air.

Josh propped an elbow on a fence post and ran a hand over the dark, bushy beard. Four months with no rules and regulations to follow with regard to shaving. For the first time in eight years, his hair touched his collar. "Maybe I don't want to be recognized."

"Oh, I almost forgot. You had some mail at the house." Matt pulled an envelope from inside the heavy duster and waved it in the air. "You keepin' secrets from me, bro? You got a girlfriend back home?"

"Nope." A shiver ran down his spine at Matt's timely question. He wished his secrets were as innocent as a girl back home. Taking the piece of mail from Matt's outstretched hand, he stuck the envelope in the back pocket of his jeans, wondering who he knew who would write a letter in this day of texts and emails. "Thanks."

"So we'll see you for dinner?" Matt leaned forward on the saddle horn and waited.

Josh had promised twice already this

month to come for dinner and had apologized by saying he had fallen asleep. He nodded. "I'll be there."

"Sounds good." Matt pulled on the reins, and his horse whirled around on his hind legs. The clatter of the hooves on the rocky hillside faded into the distance.

Josh clambered up the bank to the old ranch truck, a forty-year-old mechanical miracle. A sturdy wooden bed had replaced the original, which had probably rusted away years ago. His own truck was parked in the garage at the main house. After years of owning a vehicle for a year at the most, selling and then moving on, he had purchased a new dark green truck with an extended cab to store his things, and a short bed for anything else he might have to carry.

The job here at the MacDougal Ranch, as much as he appreciated working in the outdoors, was temporary. He just hadn't decided on his next step.

He looked around. The big cat had disappeared. He maneuvered the truck up the hill, washed in the stream, changed his shirt and jeans for the only clean pair he had and settled down by the empty fireplace to read his mail.

He ripped open the envelope. A news clipping and a piece of pink notepaper fell out. The pink paper was decorated with a picture of scissors, the Hair Today logo and Megan Martin's name.

Hi Josh, I thought you would want to see this. Text or call if you want to talk. Megan.

Josh smiled, thinking of the woman with the curly ponytail who could argue sports statistics with him all day. Neither had a romantic interest in the other, but when they had worked together backstage on the senior class play, they had discovered a common interest in sports of all kinds. He unfolded the newspaper clipping. A group of people stood in front of a business. *Why would Megan think he cared about this?*

He brought the paper closer and peered at the faces. He still didn't recognize anyone. He had been gone from home too long. He read the caption: Local Businesses Plan Holiday Party. Holly McAndrews, proprietor of The Wildflower. Now he remembered. She had been a few years ahead of him in school. Three years in a row she and her bay quarter horse had won the barrel racing contest at the county fair. He grinned at the sight of the pregnant belly. Didn't look like she was doing any barrel racing these days.

Next to Holly was Megan. And next to Megan...he did a double take, before reading the caption beneath. Suzanna Campbell, proprietor of The Cookie Jar. He almost didn't recognize his own mother. Her formerly bright yellow hair was more of a platinum blond, and she must have lost at least forty pounds. And she was using her maiden name. *What was going on?*

He took a deep breath and stared into the ashes of the old stone fireplace. He had stayed away, focusing on his own demons. Eight years as a medic, patching up his fellow soldiers, had done little to assuage his guilt about what had happened in Bear Meadows. He'd even finally gotten out of the military, hoping to find the answers elsewhere.

But the picture indicated something else was wrong. *Was his mother sick?* The weight loss... The white hair...

He was only half joking when he told

Matt he didn't want to be recognized. He had no desire to return to Bear Meadows, especially after his last visit. He had burned that bridge. What he wanted was to be left alone to sort out his thoughts. *How did the last eight years figure into the direction of the rest of his life? How would he move on from the incident that kept him away from his hometown?*

But something had happened at home. Maybe he wasn't the only one having trouble figuring out what to do next. His parents had been married twenty-five years. Didn't they know by now?

Apparently they didn't. He had to get back to Pennsylvania.

But first he had a date with a plate of lasagna.

CHAPTER TWO

"NONFAT VANILLA LATTE. And make it a double." She deserved it after the morning she'd had. Standing at The Wildflower counter, Wendy swiped her debit card and studied the woman behind the cash register. "Are you still working out? You don't look like you've gained an ounce."

Holly Hoffman McAndrews grinned as she pushed Wendy's latte across the counter. The sweet scent of vanilla wafted from the ceramic cup. "I can do limited exercise. And I walk a lot." She patted the round protrusion underneath the brown apron. "But I gave up riding horses for a while." Her smile got wider as the bell jingled over the door. "It's all his fault."

"What are you blaming me for now?" Mac McAndrews, the chief of police and Holly's husband, strode across the floor.

Wendy looked from one to the other. She may as well have been invisible.

She'd never spotted the love affair coming, what with Mac having a little girl from his first marriage and Holly thinking she wasn't the maternal type. But somehow things had worked out for the couple and, two years after they laid eyes on each other, they were a happy family, with Mac's seven-year-old daughter, Riley, and a baby on the way.

Wendy carried her cup to the low table in front of the picture window and settled into an overstuffed chair. Brown-and-yellow plaid, the colors of the local high school. Rather than go home to an empty house, Wendy had decided to research job opportunities on her laptop in the comfort of the cozy coffee shop. She would do the noon report from the bridge, with a couple shots of a still unfrozen creek, and then go home.

She sipped her latte as she waited for her laptop to connect. Ever since Holly had opened the coffee shop the previous year, Wendy had been a steady customer. She had watched Mac date a series of women, looking for the perfect partner for himself and mother for his daughter. He had even taken Wendy out to dinner, but they both knew before they finished their salads they were going in completely opposite directions.

Wendy watched the two former military members hold hands across the counter. Holly had been a great choice for Mac and vice versa. It just took them a while to figure that out.

Glancing down at the computer screen, she typed *television news jobs* in the search bar. How long would it take for her to figure things out? She couldn't stay at WSHF past January. She had to find something else. A year was long enough to wait for an opportunity. She clicked on the first listing. *Broadcast Technician, Shipboard, Worldwide. Get ready for an exciting life at sea!*

She skimmed the job requirements—which she met—and then the long list of responsibilities. The *any other job-related duties assigned* moved her finger to the delete button. She pictured herself swabbing the deck with a smelly mop. She was reading about a *TV Spot Producer* in Burbank when the bell jingled over the door.

"Hello, all, what a nice day out there with the sun shining. And there's our own weather girl to give me the latest weather report." Mrs. Hershberger, first-grade teacher to half the town, beamed her a sunny smile as she closed the door.

Wendy bit the inside of her cheek and gave the teacher a tight grin. Two times in one day. First Walt, now the teacher. The funny thing was, she believed they thought they were paying her a compliment. *Local girl makes good, and all.*

"Hello, John." The plump, recently re-tired teacher was one of the few in town, besides his mother and wife, to refer to the chief of police as John. Dropping her big purse onto the floor, she plopped into the chair opposite Wendy. "I'll try one of your special lattes, Holly. The one with pump-kin."

With a last glimpse at the Burbank job, Wendy clicked off the screen and shut her laptop. She would get no more work done with Mrs. Hershberger nearby. "Terrible storm coming in later this week, Mrs. Hershberger."

"Oh, dear, I was hoping the snow would

hold off until Christmas." The sound of the steamer filled the shop.

"Six weeks?" Wendy glanced at the coffeepot clock over the counter. If she wanted to get the remote to Walt by noon, she had better get moving. "No such luck." Her phone dinged with a message. A picture popped up on the screen. Central Park. View from Katie's window! Having a great time! The message was from her father. The photo was taken from high above the park. Obviously, her sister had an expensive apartment. She had made the big time at twenty-five, as her father never ceased to remind her.

"Wendy?"

She looked up to find the teacher staring at her expectantly. "Did you say something?"

The woman's gaze dropped briefly to the phone in Wendy's hand.

Wendy slipped the phone into her briefcase. She would save her father's exclamations of joy at being with his older daughter for later, when she had a full glass of red wine in one hand and a slice of pizza with everything but the kitchen sink on it in the other. Her mouth watered at the thought.

"I asked if Mark Murphy had done the long-range winter forecast yet."

She shook her head, partly in answer and partly to dispel the pizza image. "He's skiing in Vermont this week. The winter forecast is scheduled for next Monday's six o'clock report." Guilt over ignoring the older woman prompted her to stick with the conversation. "Are you enjoying retirement, Mrs. Hershberger?"

"I suppose." The wide smile faded. She twisted a band around her left ring finger. A single diamond winked on each rotation. "I miss the kids, and my retirement check doesn't seem to go as far as I thought it would, so I substitute when they need someone. That's why I was hoping the bad weather would hold off. My little car doesn't get around in the snow very well."

Holly chose that moment to deliver the latte. "One pumpkin spice latte. Maybe you should go to Florida, Mrs. Hershberger. My mom and dad talk about it every year but never seem to make it there."

The smile returned when Holly sank

into the chair between them. "Winters in Pennsylvania usually aren't too bad. This is my second winter being retired, and I'm just not accustomed to having so much free time."

Finishing her latte, Wendy slipped her laptop into her briefcase. She remembered the school had honored the older woman for forty-five years of teaching. Mrs. H had to be in her late sixties. *Why had she worked so long?* Everyone Wendy came across always talked about retiring as soon as possible. *Didn't Mrs. H have family? Grandchildren? She thought everybody around here had grandchildren.*

Mrs. Hershberger focused on Holly. "I read in the paper you and the other merchants are planning a holiday party and I want to hear all about it, but first…how is Riley adapting to the idea of having a baby brother or sister?"

Holly let out a burst of laughter, her green eyes dancing. She launched into a story about Riley insisting on decorating the nursery in a superhero theme.

Shaking her head, Wendy drummed her fingers on the arm of the heavily cushioned chair. At one time, Holly, world traveler, barrel racer, independent woman, had been a resource for discussing issues facing trail-blazing women in the workplace, but now she was firmly entrenched in motherhood. Holly had gone over to the dark side.

JOSH DIDN'T HIT snow until Pennsylvania. Almost a week had gone by since he'd received the letter. He wanted to finish things on the ranch before taking off, and to thank Matt's aunt and uncle for everything and to let them know he'd be back soon. Driving for twenty hours straight out Interstate 80 from Montana, he'd stopped only for coffee, snacks and gas. And once for ice cream. Water he carried in a gallon jug behind the seat. He planned to continue on with no breaks, but by the time he reached Chicago his eyes were drifting closed. He pulled off at a roadside rest stop, unwrapped his sleeping bag and pillow, and crashed for a couple hours in the cramped backseat of his truck cab.

He reached Bear Meadows late Friday. Dusk had fallen. High winds heralded the approaching storm front. The streets were dark, indicating power was out for most of the town. He considered going home, seeing his father, but concern for his mother kept him going through town to the east side, where the bakeshop listed in the newspaper article anchored one end of a five-store strip mall. He hadn't even known his mother had gone through with her plans to open a bakery and thought belatedly he should've called home more often. Once he made sure she was okay, he would stay at the family's cabin a few miles away. Facing his father would be easier after a night's sleep.

Both sides of Main Street were dark, although emergency lights in the hardware store and the bank lit the interiors. The hardware store held happy memories. Every April he and his father descended on the place, list in hand for supplies for the first day of trout season. They'd gather up their equipment, and then, with bologna sandwiches made with his mother's homemade bread and her perfectly round sugar cookies for dessert, he and his father would be on the stream at the crack of dawn. He angled his truck into the space in front of the bakery and glanced at the window in the second floor. Dark. Maybe she hadn't moved out of their home. Maybe she was using her maiden name for business purposes.

The last time he had been home his mother had mentioned taking an early retirement from the university and opening a bakery. Whenever she had brought up the subject, his father had laughed and told her to keep her day job. Obviously his mother had gone forward with her plans. Had his father's opposition forced a separation? How did the sudden weight loss enter into the equation?

For the umpteenth time, Josh weighed the possibility that his mother was sick. He would find out soon enough.

As he got out of his truck, the door was almost pulled from his hand by the gusting wind. Slamming the door, he stared at the hanging sign. The Cookie Jar. Black letters on a white background. Black and white— that was his mother. A no-nonsense kind of person.

He stomped up the snow-covered steps to the wooden porch stretching the length of the strip mall, his footprints the only disturbance in the pristine snow. He knocked lightly on the pane of glass and then turned the door handle. It was unlocked. His soldier's internal alarm sounded as he opened the door into a quiet store. The faint scent of just-baked bread filled the room. He pulled his cell phone from his inside coat pocket and turned on the flashlight app. A long pink counter filled the half of the store to his right. To his left, racks filled with loaves of bread and boxes of baked goods filled the shelves. "Mom?"

No answer. Something brushed his leg and he jerked away. A brown tail disappeared around the counter. "Another cat. At least you're small enough to handle." He followed the tail through the door into the kitchen. The old Formica table from their house occupied the center of the room. Counters covered two walls. A computer filled most of a small table in the corner near the back door. He ran a hand over the bulky monitor. "How can you keep track of a business on this antiquated thing?"

Peering into the darkness, heading for the staircase, he slowed his breathing, the better to hear if someone was in the building. Ice crystals pinged on the windows. "Mom, are you upstairs?"

No response. As he mounted the wooden steps, he stomped his boots in case she was asleep. "I'm coming up."

At the top of the staircase, he aimed the beam of light in a slow arc around the small area. A simple cot. Folded clothes in cardboard boxes on the floor. A table with a jewelry box and an alarm clock. He looked out the window at the desolate street. A basket of dried petals sat on the windowsill. He picked it up and sniffed. Rose petals. His mother had always been crazy about roses. Was she living here full-time?

He checked under the bed. No sign of the cat. Josh would have to warn his mother, a woman who had refused to allow a dog or a cat in the house, that an animal was loose in her place of business.

But he would have to find her first.

THE LONG WEEK was almost over.

Mark had returned just ahead of the big storm and, in an unexpected moment of civility, had taken the early morning show.

Wendy wasn't needed at the station until the last broadcast at 11:00 p.m.

Grabbing a yogurt container from the refrigerator and a spoon from the silverware drawer, she walked out onto the enclosed back porch. The storm she had warned Mrs. Hershberger about on Monday had indeed finally arrived. Though only late afternoon, the sky was already getting dark. Fat, fluffy flakes danced in the gathering wind. The still-green grass was almost completely covered. A blue jay chirped from the bare maple tree. She settled into the rocking chair to watch as he hopped onto a higher branch.

If her mother were home, she would be stalking the bird with a telephoto lens. But her parents had gone to New York City almost a week ago, leaving Wendy alone in the sprawling ranch house tucked back on ten acres of wooded property.

She shivered. She had dressed in comfortable sweats when she got up that morning, but maybe she needed something warmer. She settled into the chair, the only sound the scraping of the rocker

on the porch floor and the still-squawking
blue jay.

She was used to her parents going off
on some adventure or other, but she found
herself missing her mother's Yorkshire terrier, despite the insistent barking when he
wanted to be picked up. Since her mother
spoiled the bright-eyed ball of fluff, Oliver
was usually held immediately.

Not even a pet. Meaning, no dog. Ms.
King, the headhunter who'd found her the
Atlanta anchor job that had unfortunately
not happened, the woman who was still out
there searching for Wendy's big chance,
had left Wendy with a mantra. The words
echoed in her head. Oliver had filled the
need for a pet, but now he was gone, leaving her with the blue jays and cardinals in
the backyard.

She stared at the overcast sky. Mrs.
Hershberger had referred to Wendy as "our
weather girl," but the truth was, the Valentine family had been part of the Bear
Meadows population for less than ten
years. Before that, her father's computer
security business had kept them in Philadelphia, but after selling and settling into

an early, comfortable retirement, her parents had decided to move to central Pennsylvania. Wendy had been at Penn State by then and one of the few people in town the first-grade teacher hadn't taught.

Unlike her father, who had retired in his mid fifties, Mrs. Hershberger had continued to teach into her late sixties. The warm, friendly teacher would have made a great mom, possibly better than her own mother, who'd found herself pregnant at forty and not that interested in motherhood. Wendy sometimes felt her parents had been a couple so long that they forgot they had a child.

The blue jay hopped farther up the tree.

"If you had a story to tell, I'd interview you, but I think you're safe, Mr. Jay." Wendy laughed as the blue-and-white-striped bird with the crested head chirped in reply.

She had to think of something to draw the attention of the big affiliates. *Would Walt ever allow her time to interview someone? And if he did, who would she interview? Her parents?* Her parents may like living in the rural countryside of central Pennsylvania, but they craved the excitement of exotic places. *Maybe a series on unusual travel destinations?* Atlanta had been tantalizingly close. Katherine King had been as disappointed as she when the offer didn't materialize. "Keep doing what you're doing, Wendy. Try to break out from weather. It's only a matter of time."

She had tried. Last fall she had covered every game of the Bear Meadows football team. Her one attempt to dig deeper into a story had almost cost her a friendship. She had been interviewing the chief of police after some teenagers were caught stealing from stores in the strip mall. Something had prompted her to ask him about his dismissal from the Raleigh police force, which she had only come upon after looking the new police chief up on the internet. His normally pleasant demeanor had turned to stone.

Only later did she find out he had blamed himself for the death of his wife. Rather than going for milk himself, his wife had driven, unaccustomed to snow-covered roads, and crashed the car. He began drinking, and was asked to leave the police force. That was all behind him now, but no, she would not be interviewing Chief McAndrews.

She could interview the Smith brothers. Their farm was just a few miles from her parents' property. The seventy-year-old twin brothers had never married and lived on the family homestead all their lives. Two years ago they had begun selling handmade turkey calls and become an internet sensation. Skinny would be the easier of the two to interview. Hawkeye rarely said a word. Hawkeye remained a mystery. *What was his story?*

Her thoughts of potential interviewees was interrupted by the ringing of her phone from inside the house. When she jumped out of the rocker, the blue jay flew off, squawking in alarm. The phone lay on the edge of the kitchen's island countertop. "Hello?" she answered.

"I need you to do the six o'clock." No greeting, just Walt's gravelly voice.

"Where's Mark?" Glancing out the window, she noted the fluffy flakes of a few minutes earlier had increased in size and intensity. She could no longer see the garden shed from the kitchen window.

"You can do a remote."

Apparently Mark's whereabouts were none of her business. "Did you have something in mind?"

"The power's out in Bear Meadows. They're opening the church basement for people. Go there, report the weather and how people are coping. Don't try to get fancy."

"I don't have—"

"Phil will meet you. He'll do the camera work. I want him to get some shots of the roads, maybe go up to the interstate and see how traffic is moving. Then he can bring everything back for the late report."

Wendy breathed a sigh of relief. Sending the cameraman would make the assignment much easier. "Sure thing, Walt. Thanks."

"You got it, kid. Be careful driving." And without another word he was gone.

Wendy clicked off. She glanced at the cuckoo clock over the sink, a souvenir her parents had brought back after a trip to Bavaria two years earlier. She had just enough time to change, so without a moment to spare she dashed upstairs. She stared into her closet and debated the best look for outdoor reporting in a blizzard. Or should she report from inside the church? Figuring she wouldn't be outside long, she pulled on skinny jeans and a royal blue sweater. Her tall black boots and the station's monogrammed quilted jacket should get her from her car to the church basement.

Given the front-wheel drive, her car did fairly well in the snow. But who knew how quickly the roads would be plowed? The latest forecast indicated a crazy storm was on its way. And who knew that better than she?

HE TRIED EACH of the other four shops next to the bakery. A computer shop, a consignment shop, the coffee shop and finally his friend Megan's hair salon. He peered into the window and could barely make out the two chairs and mirrors. He strolled along the boardwalk, his attention now on the other side of the street. The bank and the hardware store were, of course, closed. Despite the covering of snow, he could tell the vacant lot had been renovated. Three benches were scattered among the new landscaping. This end of town had certainly improved since his last trip home.

He retraced his steps to his truck and brushed off the snow that had already accumulated on his windshield. Bank, hardware store, new park, library. Leaning on his truck bed, he studied the facade of the former carriage house that had been the home of the library for all the years he was a student. As he looked closer at the window, he could make out the design of a large cup with a thin handle. Crossing the slippery street, he glanced to his right. At the end of the street, the stoplight swung wildly in the blustery wind.

Someone had converted the old library into a tea shop. *Tea for You*. He wondered if he should try the door and then knew he would question himself if he didn't. Grasping the doorknob, he turned the handle and pushed. The door swung open. Snow blew past him and landed on the runner leading from the door to a counter. He quickly shut the door behind him. "Hello?"

At least in his mother's place of business his presence had been justified. Here, he felt like an interloper. He came farther into the room. The checkout counter had been refinished. A stained-glass lamp graced the top. Round tables and chairs were scattered through the space. Continuing through the shop, he passed a wall of loose teas in glass jars. He entered a kitchen area. The interior back door was wide open.

Josh stepped onto the back porch. Through the massive oak grove on the far side of the parking lot, the outline of the old mansion was barely visible. *Dr. Reed's home.*

One car remained in the parking lot, covered with at least six inches of snow. He remembered his father telling him the building had been a carriage house, with horses and carriages on the ground floor, while the upper floor had been living quarters for the grooms. When they created the parking lot, they had to provide a basement entrance to the original ground floor. Josh walked to the edge of the porch.

A large silver maple grew at the edge of the parking lot. One of its branches had fallen from the weight of the snow and lay squarely across the cellar doors leading to the ground floor. If anyone had been in the basement when the limb broke off, he or she was trapped. He listened. Nothing, just the skitter of snow. He could barely make out anything in the darkness until a flicker of light caught his eye. Grabbing the railing, he eased down the steps. Looking under the porch, he noticed a bit of light coming through a small cellar window. Maybe the proprietor of the tea shop had been trapped below. And maybe he or she would know where his mother had gone.

Grabbing the thick branch, he tugged. Heavier than it appeared. He pulled again and felt a pinch in his right knee. Giving his leg a shake, he grabbed the branch again and finally uncovered the cellar doors. He opened one and slid the anchoring support into the slot so it wouldn't come down on his head. Carefully descending steep stairs, he pushed open the door at the bottom and was hit with chilled air.

Boxes and supplies lined the shelves to his left. In the center of the room sat a square table, similar to the ones in the shop overhead. Lit votive candles sat on the table. Something glistened in the background. Josh stepped forward and directed his light into the recesses of the dark basement. The light landed on a brass bedpost, and then on a form on the bed, partially huddled under a quilt. He directed the light upward until he could make out a face.

"Mom?"

CHAPTER THREE

"THANK YOU, OFFICER WILLIAMS." Wendy turned to the camera and gave a curt nod. "That was Officer Robert Williams with the Bear Meadows Police Department. They have their hands full tonight. Back to you, Casey."

Phil's smiling face appeared from behind the camera. "I'm headed up to the interstate for some more footage and then to the station."

"Wendy, interview me, Wendy, interview me!" A child in purple coat and leggings ran through the deepening snow. A car door slammed.

As the little girl looked up into Wendy's face, Wendy recognized Riley McAndrews, the police chief's daughter. The girl was dressed in purple snow pants, and a matching jacket. She wore a white knit cap with cat ears made out of felt. Riley's ever-present blond ponytail bounced from a hole in the top of the knit hat, custom-made for her. "Hi, Riley. Sorry, but we're finished here. Phil has to leave."

"You *have* to interview me. I have a big story!" She tugged the fringes of Wendy's red knit scarf.

Wendy mostly knew the girl from Holly's coffee shop after school. A desk had been set up in the corner especially for Riley while Holly worked. "I'm sorry, Riley, but—"

"I have time, Wendy." With a hint of a smirk and giving Wendy no chance to respond, Phil repositioned the camera. "In three, two, one…"

The camera light blinked on.

Wendy knew Phil was a sucker for stories with kids, having two children of his own. "Okay, Riley." She positioned the girl so they both faced the camera. "I'm here with Riley McAndrews, daughter of Bear Meadows's chief of police. Tell our viewers about your big story, Riley."

The girl's light blue eyes fixed on the lens and the red light. "The baby is coming." With a tilt of her head, she smiled at the camera.

"I know. How exciting for you." Riley had spent the past eight and a half months announcing to anyone who would listen that she'd soon have a baby brother or sister. Wendy smiled back. "How old are you, Riley?"

"I'm seven years old and I'm in second grade at Bear Meadows Elementary. I'm going to be a big sister. Today." She threw out her arms and turned her face to the falling snow.

Wendy waited a beat, entranced by the child's beaming face, then remembered Phil and the camera. "Wait. You mean Holly's having the baby now? Apparently snow isn't the only big story in town. Can you share any more details with our viewers, Riley?" She crouched in the gathering snow so her face was even with Riley's. She lowered her voice to a conspiratorial whisper. "Is Holly at the hospital?"

With a sheepish grin, Riley nodded. "Holly's in labor. Daddy was supposed to work because of the blizzard, but he said he can't be in two places at one time and

Holly said if he knew what was good for him he better stay with her." Riley crossed her arms and nodded as if agreeing with her stepmother. Then she pointed at the camera.

Wendy dutifully stood and addressed the camera. "Riley's stepmother is the owner of The Wildflower Coffee Bar and Used Book Store. As I mentioned earlier, her father is the chief of police for Bear Meadows, which is busier than usual, even for a Friday night." She glanced at Riley. "Anything you'd like to add, Miss McAndrews?"

"Well—" she rubbed her chin with fingers covered with a white mitten "—do you want to know a secret?"

Not accustomed to being around seven-year-olds, Wendy couldn't imagine the type of secret the girl was about to divulge. "I sure would. What's your secret?" She held the microphone close to Riley's chin.

"I always called my daddy's new wife Holly. But the new baby will call her Mommy. So I'm thinking I should call her Mommy, too, just to avoid confusion." Blue eyes wide, Riley looked up at Wendy.

"Don't you think? Daddy said it would be okay."

Wendy threw a glance at Phil. He just shook his head and smiled. "I think that would be nice, too, Riley."

Riley bounced on the spot in satisfaction. "Good." She placed her hand over Wendy's, the one wrapped around the mike. "Can I interview you now?"

Wendy laughed. "Another time." She looked at the camera. "So ends a tumultuous evening in Bear Meadows, Pennsylvania, where the snow is piling up at the rate of an inch an hour, babies are being born and television news reporters are in the making." She wrapped her arm around the girl's shoulders and whispered in her ear.

Riley put her mittens around the microphone and stared straight into the camera. "Back to you, Casey."

Smiling at the little girl's earnest delivery, Wendy took the mike and flipped off the switch. She shot another look at Riley. "So are you staying here tonight?"

"No, Grandma and Grandpa Hoffman just stopped by to drop off ham sandwiches for everybody. We're going to the hospital because Grandpa has a big truck, and he says he can go anywhere in that truck." Catching sight of Rose Hoffman, Riley left Wendy and sprinted through the snow to her grandparents.

Wendy took in the chaos still occurring in the parking lot. Cots and blankets were being unloaded from the back of a pickup truck, and Officer Williams seemed to be all over the place, directing volunteers and those seeking shelter.

Riley ran back to Wendy. "I almost forgot," the girl said. She held out her hand. "Daddy is passing out cigars. I don't like cigars, so I'm doing Hershey's Kisses." She placed a single silver foil-wrapped candy in Wendy's palm and then ran off.

Wendy noticed just then the light on the camera blinked off when Phil slung it off his shoulder. "Wow. You just never know what kids are going to say."

"Just delete it now, Phil. I don't want to hold you up any longer."

"Delete? Are you kidding? That was great." He made to pack up his equipment. "Let's go inside and grab a cup of coffee before we take off. You know, maybe you should consider staying here tonight. Aren't your folks out of town and isn't your house pretty far out in the country?"

Wendy laughed. "A cup of coffee I'll do. But no way am I sleeping on a cot tonight."

"Josh? Joshua Orion Hunter. Is that really you?"

Great. His own mother didn't recognize him. Josh wiped a hand over his face, as if by doing so he would erase the dark beard and longish hair. "Mom, what are you doing—" he waved one hand in the direction of the candles on the table "—here?"

Suzanna Campbell Hunter threw back the quilt. She wore a pair of khakis and a white cotton blouse. "We got locked in." She glanced to her left.

Only then did Josh notice the man on the couch under a wool blanket.

His mother continued. "This is Joe Kowalsky. He owns the tea shop." She paused, took a few hesitant steps in Josh's direction, and then raced forward. "What am I thinking? Oh, Joshua, I'm so glad to see you." She threw her arms around his neck.

With a hard look at the man on the bed, Josh wrapped his arms around his mother and squeezed. He was shocked. What had happened to the soft, plump woman he remembered her being his whole life? This woman was slight and small. The mop of hair under his chin was almost white. He eased out of her tight hold and touched an errant curl. "What happened to your blond hair?"

Sue's mouth tightened, and she let out a sigh. "This is my natural color. I stopped dyeing my hair." She lifted her chin. "I only did it to please your father, and now I just have to please myself."

When Josh's gaze dropped from the almost white hair to the pale blue eyes, she stopped talking. Although Josh knew why they separated, neither of his parents had talked to him about it. He still couldn't believe his mother lived above the bakery. "How are you, Mom?"

The defiant look in her eyes dropped, and she smiled. "I'm fine, honey." There was his mother. She had one of the prettiest smiles he had ever seen. He remembered the stranger on the couch. He strode across the room, hand outstretched. "I'm Josh Hunter."

Throwing back the dark blanket, the man stood and reached for Josh's hand. He was tall and thin, with brown hair and hazel eyes. He wore a pair of rectangular black glasses. Although he didn't appear muscular, his grip was strong. "Joe Kowalsky. Your mother came down to help me carry up some supplies, and the branch broke off that silver maple in the parking lot. We were stuck. All we did was play a couple of games of checkers. Neither of us had a phone and—"

Josh held up his hand. "Why don't we hold the explanations until later? That snow out there is coming down hard. Let me get you to shelter. My truck's parked across the street."

His mother gripped his arm. "But, Josh, what are you—"

"Later, Mom." He looked around. "Do either of you have a coat?"

With a shy glance at the tall man, his mother chuckled. "I don't usually need a coat."

Josh puzzled over the faint pink flush on

his mother's cheeks. He shrugged. "Let's lock up and find out where there's shelter set up."

"Probably the church basement. They have a generator."

He blew out two of the votive candles. "Does Dad still have one at the house?" When he didn't hear a reply, he turned around.

Her mouth tight, his mother folded the quilt. He dismissed any possibility of going home. He glanced in Joe's direction. "I guess you don't have a coat, either, then."

"Upstairs. I just came down here for a minute."

"Let's make sure all these candles are out, get packed up and lock the doors." He glanced around at the stacks of sealed boxes. "I wonder if they'll have food at the church."

Joe and his mother looked at each other before Joe reached for one of the boxes. "Good point, Josh. You say you have a truck?"

"I have a cake that the Foxes ordered for an anniversary party. We'll take that, too." Sue started toward the back door.

"Wait for me, Mom, I have a light." He opened the door, and a gust of cold air blew into the basement. "Oh, by the way, I think I let a cat into your bakery."

His mother shrugged. "That's just Mister Cee." She started up the steps.

"Excuse me?"

She turned. "Cappuccino Cat. We call him Mister Cee." She disappeared up the steps into the darkness.

Josh shook his head. As if his parents' separation weren't enough of a surprise, now he discovered that his animal-avoiding mother had no problem with a cat living in the bakery. He shook his head. What else had happened in the time he had been gone?

PHIL HAD PRACTICALLY gulped down his hot coffee and had one arm in his monogrammed station jacket before Wendy could say much. She lifted her own cardboard cup of steaming coffee. "How did you finish your coffee so fast, Phil?"

He shrugged. "Working father of two. I do everything fast. See ya later, champ."

Empty jacket sleeve trailing behind him, Phil disappeared out the door.

"Wendy, would you like a ham sandwich?" Holly's mother came up to the table with a tray.

Wendy remembered Holly's mom was meant to be on her way to the hospital. "Sure. But can I help you out, Mrs. Hoffman?"

The petite woman smiled, lifted the tray and said, "Have your sandwich first, dear."

Wendy quickly bit into the sandwich, relishing the fresh bread and spicy mustard. The church basement was warm and smelled of fresh coffee. She had two bites to go when Mrs. Hoffman returned with an empty tray and sat opposite her. "Don't you have to get to the hospital?"

"I do." Mrs. Hoffman nodded toward the kitchen. "But Fritz is helping with a clogged sink." She gestured to where a pair of jean-clad legs stuck out from the cabinet below the sink. "We have plenty of time." Lowering her voice, she leaned across the table. "I was in labor with Holly for nine hours. I doubt anything'll happen before morning."

Wendy was so focused on her career, she couldn't imagine having a baby now and settling down. She finished her sandwich. "Thanks for the snack. Apart from some yogurt and my dad's snacks, I think the fridge is empty at home."

"You should stay the night. I hope somebody picks up Vera Hershberger. She's all by herself. That little house will get cold quickly."

Wendy realized if anybody knew the former teacher's history it would be Rose Hoffman, who had lived in Bear Meadows all her life. "Has she been a widow a long time?"

Mrs. Hoffman's green eyes caught her gaze and then slid away. "You should stay here tonight, Wendy. Your road probably hasn't been plowed."

Studying the older woman, Wendy could see where Holly and her three older brothers got their black hair. Mrs. Hoffman was as thin as Holly, although not as tall. Wendy tried another tack. "I was talking with Mrs. Hershberger the other day. Did you two go to school together?"

"Heavens, no. She's years older than I

am." Mrs. Hoffman pressed her lips together. "But Vera is a lovely woman. And she's been through so much." She fixed her gaze on something over Wendy's shoulder. "There's Fritz. I've got to go, dear."

Wendy zipped her coat and followed the Hoffman couple and Riley through the kitchen, into the parking lot. Someone had left a broom by the door. She grabbed it and carried it to her car, which was covered with two inches of snow in the hour she had been inside. Maybe she should consider the job in Burbank. At least she wouldn't be freezing to death. Ten minutes later most of the snow had been removed from the windshield. She returned the broom, got into the car and put on her seat belt.

She stopped at the end of the driveway and checked both directions. A looming truck idled in the street, its signal indicating it was turning into the church parking lot. She waved and pulled out. Time to go home.

AFTER WAITING FOR a small car to exit, Josh pulled into the crowded church parking lot.

The massive stone structure with its high bell tower loomed over the neighborhood. The front of the church was dark, but bright lights came from the back door. A generator ran noisily by the side of the building.

"Are you coming in?" With an anxious look, his mother placed a hand on his arm.

"No, Mom." He leaned over and kissed her on the cheek. "I'll stay at the cabin tonight. The key still over the door?"

"Oh, Josh, it's too cold—"

"I'll be fine, Mom."

Sue reached into a paper bag on her lap and slipped a package into his jacket pocket. "I'll talk to you tomorrow then."

He was about to get out and help his mother from the truck, but Joe was already assisting Sue. He would leave his mother safe at the church, but he had no intention of walking into the brightly lit crowded place. Bad enough that he was home at all. He saw a burly patrolman approach his mother and glance in his direction. It was time to make a quick exit.

He shifted into first gear and was about to take his foot off the brake when he saw the man standing in front of his truck. *How did a guy that big move that quickly?* Holding up a gloved hand, the officer rounded the truck. He tapped on the driver's window. "Sergeant Hunter?"

Josh sighed. The last thing he wanted was attention from the local police. He rolled down the window. "Yes, sir?"

"Your mom said you're home on leave from the army."

Josh didn't see the need to say otherwise. He would be gone soon. What did it matter if people thought he was still in the military? "What can I do for you, Officer?" Up close, the policeman was much younger than he had appeared at a distance. His face was round and the reddened cheeks appeared smooth. Not a whisker to be seen, as if he had shaved just minutes earlier.

"I've kind of got my hands full." One eyebrow raised with an unspoken question.

Josh knew what was coming. "I'm sorry, but I can't stay." Josh moved his hand to the gearshift lever.

The young man stuck his hand through the window. "I'm Bob Williams. Most folks call me Moose."

Removing his hand from the gearshift,

Josh gripped the other man's hand. He resisted wincing. "Is Stone still the chief of police?"

"No. He died two years ago come January. Mac McAndrews is chief now. Good man."

Josh didn't recognize the name. "Well, good luck but—"

"Mac's wife went into labor tonight." His broad shoulders lifted in a massive shrug as he grinned. "Figures, huh? And I just heard about an accident on the interstate. The plow trucks can't keep up with the snow."

Josh suppressed a groan as he felt himself getting pulled into the town's crisis. His mother's empty cabin beckoned. A quiet place in the woods. A fire in the fireplace. A shot of whiskey. A single shot.

"Look, all I need is for someone to pick up Mrs. Hershberger and bring her back to the church. She lives a block from your mom's bakery. Has a *Go Cubs* sign in the yard. She doesn't have family so…" His words trailed off.

Josh drummed his fingers on the steering wheel and pictured snow falling around the cabin, the stack of logs waiting by the door.

Moose's grin faded. "Look, man, just forget it. I've got to keep moving." He backed away.

The disappointed look on the young man's face convinced Josh he was being a heel. "Sure, Moose. I know where she lives. I'll take care of her. Don't worry." He hesitated, and then thought if he was in for a dime he was in for a dollar. "Anything else?"

"Looks like this truck of yours can go anywhere. Maybe you could check on the Smith brothers. They're two old guys—"

"Yeah, I remember. They still live on the farm on the other side of Little Bear Creek? That all?"

"I don't suppose you're familiar with Last Chance Farm. Two elderly people there, too."

Josh felt his breath catch in his chest. "I've heard of it. Anyone else?"

Moose shook his head, but his gaze was on a caravan of cars turning into the parking lot. "Thanks, man." His last words were shouted as he moved toward the new arrivals. "Your mom said I could count on you."

Josh peered out the passenger window and saw his mother outlined in the open door of the church basement. He knew she had a lot of questions for him, but then, he had a lot for her, too. Though with the man from the tea shop in the cab with them, the questions, and the answers, would have to wait. He pulled out of the parking lot and headed toward his mother's bakery. He hoped the retired teacher wouldn't recognize him, that she would be so concerned with getting to the church she wouldn't pay attention to the driver.

No such luck.

"Joshua Hunter, what are you doing here?" Mrs. Hershberger stood in the doorway of her small ranch house. Wearing a pink tracksuit, she clutched a heavy shawl draped over her shoulders.

His own mother had barely recognized him, how had the teacher? "Taking you to the church, ma'am. The power's out."

"I'll be fine here. Besides, I'm not presentable." Leaving the door open, she walked into her living room.

Hesitating, Josh looked down at the threshold. He really shouldn't be here. He stepped into the hall and closed the door. "This blizzard's forecast to continue through the night, Mrs. Hershberger. Are you sure you don't want to go over to the church for a while? If you don't like it, I'll bring you back home." Officer Williams had made a simple request, and if there was one thing Josh knew how to do, it was to follow orders.

She stood at the window, holding back the curtain so she could see. "I suppose you're right. I'll need a few minutes to get ready."

Waiting for the older woman as she gathered her belongings, he looked around the living room. The retired teacher lived comfortably, but she certainly wasn't well-to-do. The matching couch and chair were of a style at least twenty years old. An upright piano stood in one corner of the room. He walked over to look at the pictures on top. Multiple class pictures. First graders. Individual pictures of toothless children were stuck along the edges of the frames. A wedding photo. Josh picked it up. Mrs. Hershberger had been a beautiful woman, her curly hair short and dark. She wore a long white dress. Next to her stood a barrel-chested, muscular man, his hair cut in the buzz-cut style of the sixties.

"My wedding photo."

Josh jumped. He hadn't heard the woman return. Putting the picture back in its place, he turned. "Do you need a hand with anything?"

She passed him an overnight bag. "I'm ready."

Two hours later he was finally on his way to the cabin, wondering if he would be as stubborn as Mrs. Hershberger and the Smith brothers when he got old. He grinned. With his mother's and father's genes? *Probably.*

The Smith brothers had been fine, a generator rumbling outside the rear kitchen door. Although they would soon be snowed in, they wouldn't have a problem once the snowplows hit the back county roads probably in the morning. The elderly couple at Last Chance Farm had been fine as well, comfortable in the kitchen with a fire in the cookstove. They refused to go with him.

He was glad in a sense that they had the

blizzard to talk about. It took the pressure off them possibly asking more questions about why he was in town.

He slowed as he approached the turn onto the suspension bridge over Little Bear Creek. The water ran dark between the snow-covered banks, the temperature not yet having been cold enough for freezing. As he crossed the bridge, the wooden boards rumbled under his tires.

At the end of the bridge, he turned right onto the unplowed road that passed in front of the cabin. As his headlights swung in a circle, a movement caught his eye. He slammed on the brakes. The truck skidded and came to a stop.

Josh peered into the curtain of falling snow. He must have imagined it. Or maybe he had seen a deer. But no deer in its right mind would be out on a night like this. No other wildlife, either.

Still...

Leaving the truck running, he stepped out into the darkness. "Hello?" The cold wind took the word and spun it into the sky.

CHAPTER FOUR

With the flashlight app on, he pointed his cell phone in the direction he had seen movement. The combination of the heavy snow and the high winds rendered the light practically useless. He tromped to the opposite side of the bank and saw her.

She was crouching by the left rear tire, removing snow with a large broken stick, so engrossed in her task she didn't even notice his light. "Hey."

Her head jerked up. At the same time her feet went out from under her and she slipped under the bumper. Josh lunged forward and pulled her out from under the still-running car. Exhaust swirled around them. They landed in a pile of snow.

They managed to stand. She was shivering violently, but not so much that she couldn't bat at his hands as he attempted to brush snow off her shoulders. His gaze swept over her attire. Nice boots, but more suited for the runway than snowbanks. He grasped her elbow. Her boot must've caught on some obscured object because as she tried to gain her balance, she was impeded and fell forward. He swept her up into his arms.

"Whoa, there, mis…mister, I can walk." Her teeth chattering, she could barely utter the words. She elbowed his chest.

"I'm sure you can. But I don't particularly want to be out in this blizzard waiting while you take baby steps. Hang on." He hiked up the bank double-time, causing her to throw her arms around his neck. Depositing her in his truck, he returned to shut off her car.

"My family's cabin is not far from here. Do for now, okay?"

She looked like she was about to argue, but then she gave a quick nod. *He couldn't leave her out here to freeze, could he?*

Bear Meadows was determined not to leave Josh alone.

WENDY COULDN'T FEEL her toes. The thin black leather and the even thinner socks weren't doing a very good job of keeping her warm. But then again, she hadn't worn them thinking she'd be wrestling her five-year-old car out of a snowdrift. But this nice, new truck threw out tons of heat. Wrapping her arms around herself, she hazarded a glance at the stranger settling into the driver's seat and backing the truck onto the road. A fur-lined hood covered half his face and a dark beard the other, concealing his age. He could be twenty-five or forty-five.

Did she know him? Someone from the station? The shivering in her body seemed to be bouncing her brain around so much she couldn't think straight.

Maybe she should buy a truck. But she wouldn't need a truck in Burbank, right? Why was she thinking about Burbank? She didn't want to be a producer, did she? The truck eased forward. "Do I..." She had to stop and think for a minute. She lifted a hand to her frozen cheeks. Closing her eyes, she leaned her head back. "I'm... I'm... I'm so-o-o cold."

His gaze didn't waver from the white curtain before them as the truck navigated a small hill. A gloved hand reached out and wiped the condensation from the windshield. "We'll be at the cabin in a few minutes."

A spasm of alarm shot through her at the words from the bearded giant. The makeup assistant at the station had told her of a long ago incident not far from here. A man had come down from the mountains and kidnapped a girl. The FBI had actually been called in. Had the man been caught? She couldn't remember. She edged closer to the door and wrapped her fingers around the handle. She was considering launching herself into the high drifts when he made a sharp turn and the lights revealed a cozy cabin with a swing on the front porch. Somehow the swing eased her fears a bit.

"I'll go in and start a fire." The man turned and fixed her with a stare.

In the darkness of the cab, she couldn't tell the color of his eyes. Just a glint, a spark of life—

"I'll leave the truck running for heat."

Before she could answer, he opened the door, letting in a blast of wind and flurries. Just as quickly the door slammed, and she watched as his long legs ran through the deep snow and carried him up onto the porch. He fumbled around above the door and then disappeared into the cabin.

She eyed the ignition, where the fob hung from the key still inserted. Nothing personal to clue her in to the kind of man who had rescued her. No sports memorabilia, no cartoon figure. Just a black fob. She could drive away. She could drive home. The man's footprints had almost already disappeared in the rapidly falling snow. *Who was she kidding?* She again leaned her head back and closed her eyes. If worse came to worst she'd have a heck of a story. *Local Woman Captured by Mountain Man in Blizzard of the Century.* No, that was too many words for a headline. *Local Woman Disappears.* There, short, concise, attention grabbing. She smiled, pleased, then the grin faded.

Interesting story, for sure...but only if she lived to tell about it.

SHE WAS ASLEEP. Looking through the window at the young woman huddled in the cab of his truck, Josh frowned. He had no way of knowing how long she had been outside working to free her car from the snow, and she certainly wasn't dressed for the frigid temperatures. No hat. Straight dark hair curved perfectly under her chin. Bright red lipstick and heavy mascara, as if she had just come from an event. Or maybe a date. His main concern was hypothermia, followed by frostbite. She had been wearing thin driving gloves. That was one reason why he left her in the truck while he started a fire. But the heat had been too much for her.

Despite his less than friendly appearance and the fact he had brought her to a strange place, the woman had fallen asleep, her cheek pressed against the glass.

When he opened the door she fell into his arms. Which would have been fine, considering he planned to carry her through the deep snow, but she woke with the sudden movement and immediately began thrashing.

When a fist connected with his jaw, he stumbled backward. She might have made her escape then, except he had one arm half around her so as he fell he pulled her with him. For a second time, they both landed in the snow. "What the heck, lady?"

She pushed off him and blurted, "Who... who are you?"

"I—"

"And wh-wh-why did you bring me here?"

"Well—"

"I...I live across the creek, but now I'm...at this..." Finally taking a breath, she waved a hand at the cabin. "...place."

"The road is impassable on the other side of the creek." Josh propped himself on his elbows. "You're safe here...and you can get warm. I think you might have hypothermia, and if we don't get you inside, you'll have frostbite for sure."

Her gaze flicked between him, the truck and the cabin. Mumbling, she rested her forehead on her hand. The snow had already made her black jacket white.

He wasn't sure, but Josh thought he heard something about going home. Lifting himself to his feet, he held out a hand. "Do you mind if we continue this conversation inside?"

She looked at his hand. "I can walk by myself."

He withdrew. "Fine. You go on in, and I'll shut off the truck." He slammed the door and watched the petite woman lift one leg at a time from the deep snow. She teetered to one side, and he held his breath until she managed to right herself. She dragged herself onto the porch and then disappeared into the cabin.

Josh shut his eyes and lifted his face skyward. Snowflakes melted on his skin and gathered in his beard. He wished he hadn't been the one to find the woman stuck in the drift. Maybe if he had kept going, one of the snowplow drivers would have found her. But by then, she could have frozen to death.

Josh didn't want to be drawn into any small-town drama. He was still struggling with his parents and their issues. He didn't feel like he had the full story yet about his mother's weight loss, and why she and his father couldn't work things out.

Through the cabin window, he could see the flicker of the fire he had started in the fireplace. The sight might be welcome to someone else, but not to Josh. He didn't want to be here. The first glance he

had of the cabin in years made him face
the reality that the building was hardly fit
for habitation, just as his mother had said.
Maybe he should have driven her to the
church. At least the flue was clear and able
to take the smoke out into the storm. He
opened the truck door again and retrieved
the sleeping bag, pillow and his small duffel bag. He would help the lady warm up,
but first thing tomorrow he was taking her
home and going about the business that had
brought him to Bear Meadows.

Supplies under his arm, he tromped
through the snow. One foot on the first
step, he paused at the sight of a few spin-
dly branches sticking out of the pile of
snow to the left. Something new since the
last time he was home. The thorns on the
branches indicated a rosebush, and knowing his mother, he bet she had rescued an
heirloom shrub from somewhere and given
it a new home at the cabin.

Stomping his boots on the porch, he
opened the door. She sat cross-legged on
the hearth, close to the roaring fire. Working as a medic in the desert didn't give
him much experience on frostbite, but he

remembered a little bit from his training. One of the most important things was to warm the victim up slowly.

Hanging his parka on a hook by the door, he surveyed the space. The kitchen had a small fridge that, he remembered, needed a generator to run. A folded blanket, a quilt and camp supplies sat on the counter. There was an unfinished flight of stairs that led to a loft that looked out over the creek. But only two treads had been laid. The rest were stacked nearby. Obviously, his parents had stopped working on the cabin. But for now, the structure offered him and the lady a roof over their heads, protection from the winds and a fire for warmth. He had been lucky to find a pack of matches in a kitchen drawer. His gaze finally landed on the woman. Her chin rested on her chest. Walking toward the counter, he took the quilt and spread it on the floor in front of the fireplace. He lay his sleeping bag over top. She didn't move, so he rested one hand on the woman's shoulder. Her eyes flickered. She kept silent.

Josh knelt in front of her and reached for the zipper on one pretty black boot. One of the first signs of hypothermia was confusion. He glanced at her face, registering her breathing. He hoped she wasn't too far along. At some point people needed medical care.

He removed both of her boots, and then her wet socks. Her feet were ice cold. He chanced a glimpse, but she said nothing. He found a pair of thick socks in his duffel bag. When he removed her coat and took off her gloves, he noticed the tips of her fingers were white. She was going to be in pain when the blood started circulating again. *Warm her up slowly.* He checked her face for signs of distress. Dark eyelashes lay upon white cheeks. Then he eased her onto the blanket and checked her pulse. She moaned and brought her hands close to her chest.

He looked around the cabin and found a two-burner camp propane stove and a metal coffeepot. His mother had probably been coming to the cabin to get away. And from what he remembered, she wasn't often without a cup of coffee in her hand. Starting the propane heater, he poured water from the gallon jug into a pan and placed it on the stove. He was surprised to find a box of chamomile tea in a paper bag.

When the tea was ready, he carried the cup over to his visitor and jostled her shoulder. He knelt. "Wake up. You should drink this."

Her eyelids fluttered as she struggled to sit. Finally he placed an arm around her back for support. Brown eyes blinked. For the first time he noticed dark circles under her eyes. "What is it?"

"It's hot tea. Can you hold the cup?" He handed it to her. Her shivers had reduced to an occasional shudder, but she was able to wrap her hands around the mug and sip.

She should be okay. Her pulse was strong. She was alert. He had done his civic duty.

THE STINGING IN her fingers and toes woke her. Then the growling of her empty stomach. When her eyes popped open, the first thing she saw, lying on her side as she was, was a log glowing in a stone fireplace. The rest of the room was pitch-black. She pressed her fingers against her lips. Despite the pins and needles feeling, the rest of her was warm and comfortable. But she had no memory of where she was or how she got here.

Her gaze flicked upward. A single box of matches lay on one corner of the carved mantel. No clues there. A broom, the kind witches were known to fly, stood in the far corner. Her monogrammed quilted jacket from the station hung over the back of a wooden chair a few feet back from the fire, next to a small table. Her boots had been placed neatly on the floor. She wiggled her toes and could feel heavy loose socks.

Then she noticed the weight across her middle. She ran her hand along an arm wrapped in flannel. Her breath hitched as she rolled halfway over. When she saw the dark beard, everything came rushing back. The interview at the church, the coffee with Phil, the drive home with snow coming down so thick she could barely see two feet in front of her, and then just as she drove up the slight incline to the bridge, her car sliding backward into a ditch.

Her car was in a snowdrift near the bridge over Little Bear Creek. And she didn't know who had rescued her. She haz-

arded another look at the bearded face. If
he had indeed rescued her. She lifted his
arm and placed it on his hip. He continued to sleep, his breathing even. She threw
back the covers and slowly stood. Despite
the fire, the floor was freezing. She tip-
toed over to the window and looked out
on the darkness. The snow was still coming down. She could barely make out the
hulking form of the pickup. She chose the
wooden chair by the fire and took in her
surroundings.

Apparently the cabin was a work in
progress.

Her stomach rumbled again, and she remembered all she had eaten that day was a
container of yogurt and the ham sandwich
at the church. She reached around for her
coat and laid it across her lap so she could
check the pockets for food.

"I hope you're not thinking about going
back out into the blizzard."

She jumped at the words coming from
the sleeping bag. She glanced down, barely
able to make out the glint from his eyes as
they reflected the fire. "I was looking for
food."

One hand, then both arms emerged from under the sleeping bag. "You and me both. I missed supper."

"I had a ham sandwich at the church." The bearded man wore a wrinkled blue plaid shirt. The third button down hung by a few threads. She still didn't know who or what she was dealing with here. She closed her fingers around the house key in her coat pocket. If he threatened her, she could always stab him. With the house key.

"I thought you were going into hypothermia. You were a little confused earlier." He reached overhead and stretched with a loud yawn.

Somehow he didn't look as intimidating yawning. But criminals yawned. "I was?"

"Uh-huh."

She remembered considering jumping out of the truck. "I thought you were a mountain man." She looked at him. "You're not, are you?"

"A mountain man?" Leaning back on both elbows, he grinned. "No. No, I'm not a mountain man."

"But I don't even know who you are."

His smile grew wider. "We're even then."

She waited. But Walt's journalist trick didn't work on this guy. He didn't seem to be much of a talker. "My name is Wendy."

Even white teeth flashed from the dark beard. "Nice to meet you, Wendy. Did you have any luck with those pockets?" She looked down at the coat in her lap. Her fingers still clutched the house key. She flexed her fingers and felt something else. Withdrawing her hand, she held up Riley's baby gift. "One Hershey Kiss. Want to split it?"

He laughed, a deep, rumbling laugh and suddenly she felt better than she had since he had pulled her from underneath the car. "You need the energy more than I do." Crawling onto the floor just as she had minutes before, he stood. "I'll see if I can find something to go with a single Hershey Kiss."

Ten minutes later she sat on the chair, the quilt around her shoulders. Coffee bubbled in the glass top of an old-fashioned percolator tucked close to the fire. Using one of his gloves as a hot pad, Josh picked up the pot and poured each of them a coffee. "I have no idea how old this coffee is." He walked over to where his coat hung on a hook by the door and reached into a pocket. When he returned he handed her a cookie and placed the bag between them.

Wendy picked up the mug covered with pink roses and sipped. "Is this your cabin?"

His mug was dark green with the words Army Mom on the side. "Belongs to my family."

Funny, but she didn't remember ever seeing the man across from her around town. She set down her cup, reached for a cookie and took a bite. "Not bad. Try one." The man carried homemade sugar cookies around in his coat pocket. The treat reminded her of something, but she couldn't recall what. Her mother certainly wasn't a baker, even during the holidays. She watched the man, roughly her own age, she decided, devour his cookie in two bites. "You must be starved. You can have the rest. I'm still working on this one."

"No, we share. That's fair." He reached for another cookie. "But I don't think I've ever seen anyone eat a cookie as slowly as you."

"My father says I eat slowly because I like to savor my food." She smiled, thinking of her parents' exasperation with her dawdling over dessert as a child.

"Speaking of parents, aren't yours worried about you? I grabbed your purse from the car. Maybe you should call somebody? A boyfriend? A coworker, even."

Wendy laughed at the thought of calling Phil away from his family. Only then did Wendy notice her purse next to her boots. Reaching over, she searched the contents for her phone. She held the screen next to the fire to see. "Dead. I was wondering what time it is."

"Oh dark thirty."

Smiling at his response, she dropped the phone back in the purse. "No boyfriend. And my parents are away, not that they would notice. Dad is with his other daughter. His favorite." She forced a smile and decided to change the subject. She held up the rose cup. "Seems like an odd choice for a manly man such as yourself."

He laughed. "That's my mom's."

She took a deep breath and felt a little better. Although plenty of serial killers had mother issues. "This has been quite the adventure." She tilted her head toward the back corner of the room. "What's behind that door?"

The man twisted to see where she was looking. "The bathroom. Green."

"Green?"

"Compostable."

"Oh. Well, at least there's a bathroom."

"I have my priorities." His grin disappeared when he picked up the two remaining cookies. "You should eat these. Your body needs to manufacture heat to make up for your drop in body temperature."

"I'll make you a deal. I'll eat one more if you eat the other." She held up the Hershey Kiss. "And we split this."

His teeth flashed behind the beard. "Deal."

She picked up the tiny pyramid of chocolate, bit off half and handed her companion the remainder.

"Thank you."

She shivered. The half of her body next to the fire was warm, but the other half was freezing.

"You should get back under the blanket. This cabin wasn't intended for winter oc-

cupation." Taking her empty cup with the
roses, he carried both over to the counter.

Wendy slithered under the covers and
rolled over so she faced the fire. She heard
him use the bathroom, then walk over to
the chair that she'd just vacated. A heavy
silence filled the room. Military. Oh dark
thirty was a military reference. She shivered again.

"Still cold, huh?"

"I can't sleep," she whispered.

"Me neither. Must be the caffeine in the
coffee." Josh shifted in his seat, staring
at the fire. "I could go for a bowl of ice
cream."

Wendy rolled her eyes. "There's a blizzard right outside that door, and you want
ice cream?"

"I love ice cream." He smiled. "What
would you have?"

She stared up at the ceiling and again noticed the inaccessible half-built loft overhead. "Pizza." Her stomach growled as if
in response to her words. "Pizza with everything on it."

"You haven't lived until you've had pizza
in Italy."

"You've been to Italy?"

He nodded. "Fresh, locally grown ingredients."

For the first time, she noticed the striking color of his eyes, a brilliant blue. What she could see of his cheeks above the beard and his forehead looked tan.

He dropped his gaze to hers. The blue eyes grew wary. "What are you staring at?" His brow creased, as if uncomfortable with her scrutiny.

"You work outdoors."

His eyes narrowed and focused again on the fire. He seemed to struggle with his response. "Montana."

Wendy nodded. "Thought so. You're a cowboy."

Crinkles appeared at the corners of the blue eyes. "Yep, I'm a cowboy. My name's Josh."

"So what are you doing in Bear Meadows, Cowboy Josh?"

The crinkles disappeared. "Checking on my mom." He threw her a look. "Are you sure your phone's dead? You should check it again. Maybe you can call someone now."

She huffed out a breath. "Doubt it. And like I said, my parents are visiting my sister and staying until after Thanksgiving. They wouldn't notice I was gone even if they were home. One time after church I left the sanctuary, this is when we lived in Philly, and I went into the social hall with my friends. My parents were halfway home before they noticed I wasn't in the car."

Josh laughed. "Poor baby."

"Tell me about it. My parents are all about each other. I'm just in the way."

"Well, at least yours love each other. My parents can't be in the same room together without arguing."

Interesting. Her reluctant talker was beginning to open up. Score one for a fireplace and a sleeping bag. "Two opposite scenarios, and yet neither of us is happy. What's up with that?"

Instead of answering her question, he asked, "So, no boyfriend?"

She frowned. "A boyfriend doesn't figure into my career path."

He rubbed his hands together by the fire. His fingers looked rough, which made sense. He was a cowboy. She met his gaze, though neither of them spoke.

Finally, Wendy broke the silence. "You know, usually when I like someone, I know his last name."

He leaned down until their lips were just inches apart. "Consider this a new adventure."

CHAPTER FIVE

THE CABIN WAS bathed in soft, white light when Wendy woke later that morning. All that remained of the large log was a small black chunk surrounded by glowing coals. She felt oddly at peace, more peaceful than she had felt for a long time. Then she remembered the look, and saying she liked him. The gentle, warm grin, after which she fell fast asleep. *What had she been thinking?*

Katherine King's words echoed in her mind. *No men, no kids, not even a pet.* Katherine King, the headhunter who had found her the job in Atlanta that had unfortunately fallen through, the woman who was still out there looking for Wendy's big chance. Wendy had obeyed Ms. King's advice. She didn't count the dinner with Mac because the evening had gone exactly nowhere.

She rolled out of the sleeping bag onto the cold floor. Grabbing her boots and jacket, she rose and walked over to the window. She squinted at the glare from the sun shining off the new snow. At least the snow had stopped falling. She could make out the water of Little Bear Creek just beyond the trees. Above was the bright blue of a winter sky. Josh's coat hung next to hers on a hook. She glanced down at the pocket and thought about borrowing his truck. Squeezing the left pocket, she felt the sharp edges of the key.

"You're not going to steal my new truck, are you?"

She jumped, and then glanced over her shoulder. "Who, me?"

Josh smiled. "Because I can't let you do that. I just got her."

"Her?"

"My new truck."

Even from this distance she could see the intense blue of his eyes. Looking away, she went to the counter. "Of course not." Unlike the front window, which overlooked the road, and then the creek to farm fields on the other side, the window above the sink looked out on a steep bank covered with pine trees and mountain laurel.

"I could use some breakfast. Scrambled eggs with onions and green peppers, sausage and bacon..." He groaned. "Sugar cookies and half of a Hershey Kiss just don't do it for me anymore, you know?"

She had forgotten the intimacy of the night before. She had awakened, freezing, and he had made coffee. She wasn't comfortable with the familiarity. "If you would be so kind as to take me home, perhaps I can find something to feed you."

His grin faded. "If I would be so kind..." He struggled to his feet. He'd slept near her, also close to the fire, and used the quilt for warmth. Picking up the quilt, he rolled it in a ball and left it on the wooden chair. "Certainly, *mademoiselle*."

He checked the fire and then, satisfied it was safe, got his coat from the hook. He opened the door.

Wendy's breath caught at the sight greeting them. A foot of snow had blown against the front door. "Can your truck make it? It looks pretty deep."

"We'll find out, won't we?" He grabbed

the broom from the corner and shot her a look. "Finish getting ready, and I'll clean off the truck."

She nodded. Her socks and boots were dry. She removed the heavy socks and replaced them with her own. She zipped up her boots and slipped on her jacket, then went over to the window. The truck was cleared of snow. She took a deep breath and stepped onto the porch.

Josh leaned the broom against the porch and locked the door. Reaching in his pocket, he replaced the key on the ledge over the door.

So the sharp object in his coat pocket hadn't been the truck key after all. She'd forgotten about the fob. Good thing she wasn't planning on making a run for it.

"Do you want some help?" He glanced from the porch to the truck. Melting snow ran down the windshield and plumes billowed from the truck's tailpipe.

Her gaze followed his. The snow was as high as the porch. But she had already depended enough on the stranger…er, Josh. "I can do it." She threw him a glance. "I'll follow in your footsteps."

"Okay." He sounded doubtful, but she managed it. It wasn't until they had gotten to the main road and the bridge did the conversation resume. "Looks like they made one pass through here this morning." He pointed to the other side of the road, where they could barely see the red roof of her car. "You'll have to call a tow truck. Cross the bridge, you said?"

"Yes, then turn right."

"Right? Down Last Chance Road?"

"Yes." Wendy studied her rescuer's profile. She had detected a note of tension in his cryptic response. "Is that a problem?"

"No." He looked out the window. "I only know of one farm down that road. I thought maybe you lived past the Smith farm."

"Well, we haven't been there long. My parents built a house a few years ago. I was attending Penn State, my dad had retired and they decided they liked the area. I commuted from home."

Josh nodded. "Lucky you."

"For sure." She pointed to a mailbox by the side of the road. "Turn here." The long driveway had already been plowed and was cleared so well she could see bits of the blacktop through the layer of snow. "My dad must have someone set up to plow the driveway."

"Nice."

"Pull around back."

The parking area there was plowed, but the short sidewalk was not. Wendy appreciated how Josh grabbed the snow shovel by the back door and cleared the pathway. She went in via the kitchen door, turned up the heat and made coffee. Her phone had completely died, so she plugged it in to recharge.

She was checking the refrigerator when she figured it out. *Of course.* She heard the kitchen door open and close. She turned. Josh stood just inside the door looking around the modern kitchen.

"Well, I guess you're good so…"

"I made coffee. I owe you that much and something to eat." She pointed to the booth next to the window, where two steaming cups of coffee waited. "Have a seat, Mr. Hunter."

His eyebrows shot up until they disappeared in the thick mop on top of his head. "Excuse me?"

"That's your name, right? You're Josh Hunter, Sue Hunter's son." Wendy crossed her arms in satisfaction at the look of shock on the young man's face. *Ha! Was she an investigative reporter or not!*

"You are correct." He settled into the booth and stared out the window. "Your bird feeder's empty."

Wendy's arms dropped to her sides. "Don't you want to know how I guessed your name?"

He shrugged.

So much for that. Her phone dinged. She had a message from Walt. *Call me.* She pulled a box from the freezer. Walt would have to wait until she fed her unexpected company. "I don't cook much here, but my dad has some breakfast sandwiches in the freezer. Will that do?" She glanced over her shoulder. "Josh?"

A faint flush appeared on his cheeks. "That's fine." He seemed uncomfortable, whether from being in her house or at her figuring out his name, she wasn't sure. "Is that your dog?"

"I don't have a dog." Wendy watched the timer click down on the microwave. "My mom has a terrier, but she took him with her." The microwave dinged. She set one egg and muffin sandwich in front of Josh and kept one for herself. Suddenly starving, she quickly sat opposite him at the table.

He sipped his coffee and looked down at his food. "Okay, but there's a dog in your yard. And he looks cold."

She peeked out the window just in time to see a big black dog lift his leg against the maple tree. Her mother wouldn't be happy about that. With a longing glance at her cooling breakfast, Wendy jumped up and opened the door, intending to shoo the animal away. Instead he slipped past her as if he had done so hundreds of times, shook, scattering wet snow in every direction, and curled up on the rug in front of the sink.

"He has a lot of nerve." She thought she saw Josh grin as he held his coffee cup to his lips.

"He doesn't look too bad. Maybe he took shelter on your porch."

Wendy knelt. "He has a collar but no tag."

"Looks like you have yourself some company while your parents are gone."

Wendy's heart jumped into her throat. *No men, no kids, not even a pet.* And here she was with a man and a dog. If she weren't careful, she'd soon be building a snowman with a passel of kids in the backyard.

JOSH WONDERED AT the look of alarm on Wendy's face when he suggested she keep the dog. She obviously wasn't afraid of the creature. So what was the big deal? "You don't like dogs?"

"Of course I like dogs." She sat back on her heels. "I used to have a dog like this one a long time ago. Her name was Maggie." She ran a hand over the animal's smooth dome. The dog rolled over. When she didn't respond, he nudged her knee with his nose.

"Looks like he has your number."

She smiled, and then the smiled faded. "Why don't you take him into town, Josh? He's lost. Somebody will know where he belongs."

"No way." Josh held up his hands, palms out. "I've only been back twice since high school. I don't really know anybody. Besides, I'm not going into town. I'm heading to the cabin." His sandwich already gone, he slid out from the booth, dragging his coat behind him. "Thanks for breakfast."

Concern lit her eyes when she glanced up. "You'll be cold there. And you don't have anything to eat."

He gave the woman and dog a wide berth on his way out. It was past time for him to go. He pulled open the door and took a deep breath of the frosty air. "I'll be fine."

"Wait." Wendy jumped up from the floor so quickly the dog skittered under the table. She looked from the dog to Josh. "At least let me give you some food to tide you over. We don't have a lot, but still…"

Josh waited. He was afraid if he let go of the door handle he might want to stay. Get to know her better. He gripped the knob tighter, watching Wendy throw bread, cold meat, snacks and cans of soda in a basket she brought from the laundry room.

Finally, she propped her hands on her hips and tried to catch his gaze. "Thank you."

Josh avoided her eyes, his gaze on the dog, still under the table. "Nothing to thank me for, miss. I just did what anybody would do."

She came closer. "Miss? What happened to *mademoiselle*?"

He heard the note of teasing in her voice, but even so, his body tensed at her close proximity. When he tore his gaze from the dog, he looked into her soft brown eyes. Only now did he see the flecks of amber. For some reason they reminded him of the mountain lion he had seen in Montana, whether because of the color or the unblinking stare he couldn't say. He had to clear his throat before he could answer, but even so, the words came out softly. "I don't know."

Resting her hands on his shoulders, she stood on her tiptoes and kissed the one bare spot high on his cheek. "Thanks for…for… uh, warming me up." Her face reddened at the memories her words evoked. "I mean, uh, never mind. If I can ever return the favor…"

"You don't owe me anything." His fingers released the doorknob, compelled of their own volition to cup her cheek, warm and soft.

She rested her hand on his chest, fingering the loose button. "Josh, last night was—" she bit her lip, as if uncertain what to say "—kind of special. But when I said I didn't have time for a boyfriend, I meant it. My work, well…" The button fell into her hand.

"No need to tell me, Wendy." He withdrew his hand from her cheek and reached again for the doorknob. "I'm not planning on sticking around town any longer than I have to." He stepped out onto the back porch.

"Wait."

He turned. "Yes?"

"Your food." Tucking the button into her pocket, she handed him the laundry basket. He took one last look at her and then he was gone. Seconds later he was in his truck, speeding away.

When he crossed the bridge, he started to turn right onto the lane that would take him to the cabin. Instead, he slammed on the brakes, spotting Wendy's red car. *Should he go back to her? They did have a connection…he thought.* But he had to remember why he was back in town. He had seen his mother, oddly chummy with the tea shop owner. He had yet to see his father.

He turned left.

Ten minutes later he stood in the kitchen of his childhood home. "What happened to all the furniture?" The last time he was here, his mother's matching couch, chair and end tables had flanked the television. His mother prided herself on having a comfortable and attractive living room. Now the space was empty, but for his dad's large recliner and a giant-screen television. "Where's Grandma's rocker?"

Brad Hunter stood at the stove. He had been in the middle of making lunch when Josh arrived. Instead of a hug, his father had offered to cook him a hamburger. Nothing had changed. Brad Hunter was not a demonstrative man. "In your bedroom."

When no more information was forthcoming, Josh decided to set the table with the ketchup and rolls. "Soda?"

His father's grunt indicated an affirmative. He had brought Wendy's laundry basket into the house, figuring the cold meat would fare better in a refrigerator than the cabin. He retrieved two cans of soda, noting that Wendy's family liked cherry-flavored cola just as he did. Brad turned off the stove and set a plate of hamburgers on the table. He pulled a large bag of potato chips from the top of the refrigerator.

The next few minutes were taken up with the snap of opening cans and fixing the burgers. His dad poured a healthy serving of potato chips on his paper plate and waved the bag at him. "Chip?"

"Thanks." Josh hadn't realized how hungry he was. Except for the breakfast sandwich and the cookies, he hadn't eaten since noon the day before. Ketchup dripped from the sandwich down the front of his shirt. He dabbed with a paper towel, then decided the effort was fruitless. "Mind if I take a shower later?"

"Help yourself. Your clothes are still in the drawers. They'll probably even fit."

"Thanks."

"You're welcome to stay, too." His father leaned back in his chair. "So what brings you home?"

Anyone else might have been insulted at his father's question. Josh didn't answer until he finished the last bite of his second hamburger. "I don't understand what's happened. Is Mom sick? Is that why she moved out?"

Brad's head jerked at his question. "What?"

"Mom. Is she sick? She must have lost about forty pounds." Josh tapped one finger on the surface of the cheap wooden table. What happened to the old Formica one? And then he remembered. The original kitchen table was in the cooking area of his mother's bakery. "Does Mom have cancer?"

Brad's eyes popped open. "What? No, of course not." He pushed a broken chip around on the paper plate. "At least, I don't think so."

"You don't think so? You don't know if your wife has cancer or not?" Josh's voice rose at the end.

Brad pushed back his chair and stood, his face red. "How should I know? She never talks to me." He tossed his paper plate into the garbage can and stood looking out the window over the sink.

"I'm sorry." Josh stood and put a hand on his father's shoulder. "I'm worried about her." His father turned, and Josh caught the dejected look in his father's eye. "About both of you."

"Have a seat. I'll try to tell you." Rummaging in a cupboard, his father brought a box of cookies to the table. "Help yourself."

Josh glanced at his father, expecting an explanation, but none came. "You're eating store-bought cookies?"

Brad grimaced. "Your mother won't be baking for me anymore, son."

Josh's stomach churning had nothing to do with the two hamburgers and can of soda he had consumed. "What's going on, Dad?"

CHAPTER SIX

HER CAR WAS delivered quicker than she expected. Apparently she was the only person in town to have ended up in a ditch thanks to the blizzard because the two tow truck drivers were thrilled with the job and her generous tip.

Having changed into jeans and a sweater, she had been reading the paper in front of the fire when the black dog wandered into the den. He seemed perfectly at home. She scratched behind his ear. "I've got my car back, and I have the weekend off. Now what do we do about you?" Except for the brown nose and brown toes, the dog could pass for a brother of her childhood pet. So she knew he was at least part Lab.

With a low moan, the dog rested his chin on her knee and stared up at her.

Wendy tossed the paper on the couch. "If I leave you in the house while I drive to town to find your owner, will you be okay?"

In response, the Lab stretched out at her feet, legs splayed in opposite directions, and rested his muzzle between his paws.

Wendy laughed. "Somebody spoils you." He was a handsome dog, his hair shiny black. As much as she would've liked having a dog around the house, she knew it was only a matter of time before she left the area, and she wouldn't have time for a pet. Just like Katherine King told her. It didn't seem fair. And leaving a second dog with her parents was out of the question. "I know. The Wildflower. That place is like Grand Central Station on Saturday mornings. Someone there will know about a missing dog."

After walking the dog around the yard so he could do his business, Wendy left the animal stretched out in the den and drove into town. The Wildflower was busy when she got there, as if the brief snowstorm had made people stir crazy. Everyone wanted to get out of their houses. The Wildflower, with its delicious scent of fresh-roasted coffee beans and just-baked cookies, was the perfect destination. Louise Williams's curly blond locks appeared just over the top of the cash register. "I heard Holly went into labor last night. Did she have the baby?"

Louise's red lips parted in a wide smile. "A boy. I'm so happy. Now her little boy and mine will be best friends, just like Holly and I have been since kindergarten."

"Skinny vanilla latte, Wendy?" Carolyn, wife of Holly's oldest brother, Sonny, stood at the espresso machine, her rich auburn hair pulled back with a huge clip.

"Please. And a cranberry scone, heated." She swiped her debit card. "I'm surprised to see you, Louise. Your baby isn't very old."

"His two-month birthday was yesterday. Bob and R.J. are getting in some father-son time." Her blue eyes twinkled.

Wendy couldn't help remembering Louise as a young widow just three years earlier. While Louise worked in the emergency room late one night, her husband had been brought in after an accident on the interstate. After a period of self-imposed isolation, she had agreed to help Holly when she opened the coffee shop. When she met

Bob "Moose" Williams, despite him being younger in age, she found love a second time and became her old self. "I thought you were starting back at the hospital."

"Not until spring." She looked over Wendy's shoulder. "Hi, Deb. Soy latte?"

Wendy moved to the end of the counter as the mayor and former real estate agent placed her order. The Wildflower was certainly buzzing. Waiting for Carolyn to finish preparing her drink, she looked around the room, wondering if any of the Bear Meadows residents had the story that might propel her to television news stardom.

Bill, the town's mailman, waited patiently in one of the four cushioned chairs. He and Deb must still be an item. Hardly news. Next to him Mrs. Hershberger relaxed, a magazine on her lap.

"Here you go, Wendy." Carolyn gave her a quick smile. "Hey, nice interview, by the way."

"Excuse me?"

"Your interview with Riley was on the eleven o'clock news last night. Adorable." Carolyn's eyes widened in alarm as she looked over Wendy's shoulder. "Freddy, be careful. Rosalyn, don't let your brother climb the bookshelves." She rounded the counter and made a beeline for the alcove.

Still in a state of shock at the news Walt had run the interview, Wendy picked up her latte and scone and searched for a seat.

The couch was occupied by customers, including Carolyn's younger brother Chris. Wendy thought Chris was the best looking of the three brothers, but then, she had always been attracted to the neat, trendy style of the young pilot. The rocking chair and beanbag in the magazine corner were taken over by Sonny's twin daughters and son, and Chris's toddler. His wife dressed Harley in the latest fashion so that the little girl always looked like a model, just like her mother, only in the baby category. It was too cute. "Hi, Chris. Home for a visit, I see. Where's Valerie?"

The only empty seat in the room was the one near the retired teacher, the mailman and the mayor. Wendy carried the plate and cup over to the table. If anyone knew what was going on in this town, these three would.

"Oh, hey, Wendy. She's getting a massage. Mom hired a masseuse on weekends." He crossed his legs and ran a hand down the crease in his dark jeans. His tasseled loafers were spotless, as usual.

"The Flowers' B&B is really coming up in the world." She took off her coat and threw it over the back of her chair.

"Give us a plug on your next weather forecast."

Wendy laughed and sat, anxious now to dig into the warm scone.

"Bill and I are getting a couple's massage later." Deb Gold elbowed the postal worker.

Bill blushed. "She talked me into it."

Suddenly Wendy remembered the reason she had driven into town. "I had a black dog show up at our house this morning. Is anyone missing a dog? He looks at least part Lab."

The couple shook their heads. Mrs. Hershberger paused while sipping a latte. "Fran Collier has a black Lab. Daisy. Do you think it's her?"

Wendy pictured her new boarder lifting his leg against the maple tree. "I don't think so." She forked off another bite of scone.

Deb leaned over the arm of her chair

to address the Hoffman brothers. "By the way, boys, I thought you might want to know I've decided to sell my father's classic car."

Sonny quit topping up his brother's coffee mug as his brow shot up. "Dr. Reed's pride and joy? After all these years?"

"It's a gas hog, for one thing. And for another, it should be appreciated by someone who likes old cars. It hasn't been driven since my father passed away, and even then, he and the caretaker were the only ones who drove it."

"I'll take—"

"Don't even think about it, Sonny!" Carolyn called out to her husband from her spot behind the espresso machine.

Sonny spread his arms wide in mock confusion. "Who? Me? What would I want with a classic car in mint condition?" He threw a grin at his brother. "No, although moneybags here might be interested."

"The thought is tempting, but we're just too busy right now, Deb."

"Thanks anyway, fellas." Deb stood. "Ready, Bill?"

"What about the mansion?" Chris asked.

Deb shot the airline pilot an appraising look. "Do you and Valerie want to turn it into a B&B? We could use another one in town."

Chris laughed and shook his head. "My wife would kill me. Your father's house is so beautiful, it's a shame to let it sit empty."

A mixture of regret and sadness crossed the former real estate agent's face for just a moment before she brightened. "You have a point, but I'm not quite sure about what to do with it yet. See you later, folks."

"Have fun." Wendy watched the couple leave. Through the window she saw Bill reach for Deb's hand as they crossed the street. "I guess you're never too old to fall in love."

Mrs. Hershberger nodded. "That's true. I'm happy for them." But her voice was weak.

"Are you okay, Mrs. Hershberger? Can I get you anything? This scone is delicious. Would you like one?" This was the first time she had encountered the older woman seeming depressed. She was always the first to put a positive spin on any situation.

"No, thanks, dear. I'm a little blue today.

My husband's in the hospital. The house is so quiet without him I came here for some company." She glanced at the children giggling in the alcove. "And some noise."

"I didn't realize. I'm sorry to hear that about your husband. I don't believe I've ever met him." Wendy followed the teacher's gaze to the children. Sonny's twins must be in fifth or sixth grade. One of the girls was reading to her little cousin. However did they tell them apart? "Do you have children?"

"Hank and I were never blessed that way. I guess my students have been my children." She nodded toward the young Hoffmans.

"I've been told you were a great teacher," Wendy said.

"She got an award when she retired last year. And the senior classes were always naming her as favorite teacher." Louise chimed in from her vantage point at the cash register.

The single diamond in her wedding band glinted in the light as the teacher waved her hand in the air emphatically. "They were good kids. Every one of them."

"And she went to Antarctica last year. I'll bet you have some good stories about your trip." Carolyn retrieved dirty cups from their table and headed toward the kitchen.

Wendy chewed thoughtfully, wondering what Walt would think about an interview with the teacher. Probably only if Wendy could tie it to the weather. She studied the teacher, who had returned to her magazine, and wondered what her own sister would think of interviewing a retiree who everybody in town thought was the best teacher ever. Katie Valentine probably wouldn't waste her breath. She would be out there looking for someone with a real story to tell. A big story.

Wendy finished the scone and picked up her cup. Time to go home and take care of the dog. The weekend stretched ahead of her. Then she realized she hadn't returned Walt's call.

"WHY DIDN'T YOU tell me?" Josh ran his palm over the smooth white surface of the old Formica table. Specks of gold were scattered across the surface. He sat in the kitchen of his mother's bakery while she washed dishes. Dinner rolls baking in the oven filled the room with a delicious smell. Five dozen would soon be on their way to the nursing home for the Sunday evening meal.

"And exactly when should I have mentioned your father initiated divorce proceedings so he could go to Colorado with his new girlfriend? During one of your many phone calls?" His mother lifted a hand dripping with soap suds in the air. "Oh, wait. You don't call. That's right." She rinsed the large mixing bowl and set it to dry in the dish rack. "Or maybe on one of your many visits home? Oh, that's right—"

"The girlfriend is out of the picture now. Things have changed. You've changed, too, Mom."

She turned, reaching for a dish towel to wipe her dripping hands. "I've changed? So it's okay for your father to have an affair, but it's somehow not okay for me to start my own business?" She turned back to the sink.

But not before Josh saw the tears in her eyes. "No, of course not." He dropped his head in his hands and thought of Wendy complaining about her parents' behavior. *Which was worse? Being ignored by your parents or being pulled apart between them?* After leaving his father the day before, he had returned to the cabin, intending to read a few college admission books he had collected over the summer. But his attention kept returning to Wendy, he wondered if she was as lonely as he. He needed to shut down those thoughts, which was why he was visiting his mother on a busy Sunday morning.

His mom set two mugs of coffee on the Formica table with a plate of chocolate chip cookies before sitting across from him. "Are these still your favorite?" The tears had already dried, and her voice was normal.

Josh stuck a whole cookie in his mouth. "You bet." His words came out jumbled, but his heart lightened when he saw his mother's smile. Sure, his mother knew about the girlfriend, but she didn't know his dad's girlfriend had sold his mom's furniture to her sister, bought new and then taken it all with her when she left. *One thing at a time.*

"I'm going upstairs to change. I won't be long." She twirled her cup on the table. "Will you be here when I get back?"

"Sure, Mom, I'm not going anywhere." He reached for another cookie. His heart broke at his mother's disconsolate look. He wasn't going anywhere right this minute, but he wasn't staying in Bear Meadows any longer than he had to.

"Take the rolls out if the timer goes off before I come down, okay?" Taking her coffee with her, his mom went up the back stairs.

Listening to her moving around up there, Josh refilled his cup, emptying the pot. He wondered if his mother had drunk most of the pot herself. That could explain part of her jitteriness and even some of her weight loss. She was living on caffeine.

He stood in the doorway of the kitchen and looked into the shop. The space wasn't very big, which probably accounted for the fact she had no seating. He wondered if people would stick around if they had a place to sit, and then realized his mother didn't want people to stick around. His father's affair must have been mortifying for her. The timer dinged. Josh moved just as his mom entered the room. "Wow." His jaw dropped.

His mother wore a sleeveless black dress with a silver buckle at the waist. She had brushed her almost white hair neatly back from her face, which made her light blue eyes all the more noticeable. "Can you get the rolls?"

Josh didn't move from the doorway. "Are you wearing lipstick?"

"For goodness' sake." His mom rushed across the room, grabbed an oven mitt and removed the tray of rolls from the oven. She placed the tray on a rack to cool and turned off the oven. Finally, she faced him.

"How much weight have you lost, Mom?"

She hung the towel on the rack. "How would I know? I don't have a scale." She propped her hands on her hips.

Josh took a breath. He would rather negotiate with a pair of mountain lions than with his parents, and would probably have more luck. He sat down. "I don't want to argue, Mom. I'm worried about you." He patted the chair next to him. "Please. Sit."

Instead, she carried her cup to the coffeepot. "You finished it?"

"I only had one cup. You had the rest."

Sue set her cup in the sink and then sat next to Josh. She pinched his cheek. "Is this beard a permanent thing? I can't see your handsome face." She smiled.

"Maybe." Josh held her hand between both of his. "Have you been to the doctor lately?"

Sue's brow wrinkled. "Yes, I suppose. For the usual stuff."

"I mean…" Josh took a breath. This was harder than he thought. "I mean, have you been checked out? Weight loss isn't normal, and you seem to be overheated a lot."

Sue chuckled.

"This isn't funny, Mom. Are you having night sweats?"

She nodded. "As a matter of fact I am."

Josh's heart lurched. He was onto something. He just prayed the illness wasn't cancer. "Mom, you've got to go to a doctor. As soon as possible."

"I wish you had become a physical therapist like we planned, Josh. Or even a doctor. You always had such an interest in medicine. Dr. Reed had high hopes for you."

"Let's not go there, Mom. That's water under the bridge."

"If your father hadn't been so insistent on you helping him with the landscaping business, you would have been able to concentrate on your studies. You wouldn't have been so distraught. But no, he made college into a debate like he does everything. It's his fault you flunked out your first semester. He ruined everything."

Josh doubted his mother would be open to a reconciliation once she knew the truth. But his parents' marriage was nothing compared to her health. "You should see a doctor, Mom."

"I did, son."

"And what did the doctor say?" His heart thumped in his ears. First his father admits to cheating, then the talk of divorce and now cancer. His past mistakes had brought bad karma down on his family. It just wasn't fair. He tightened his grip on her small hand. "What did he say, Mom?"

"She said—" his mother smiled "—I'm going through early menopause." She squeezed his hands before pulling away. "I guess you haven't encountered that diagnosis with your soldiers, hmm?" She jumped up. "I'd love to chat about my personal medical history, Josh, but I've got to go."

Josh leaned back in his chair. His mother was right. He had never given menopause a thought. "Well, uh, that's great, I guess."

"Yes, I'm getting old. Yippee." His mother grabbed a purse, her heels echoing through the shop. "Come on, son. You're such a slowpoke."

Grabbing his coat, Josh followed his mother out the door. "What about the rolls?"

"They have to cool." Winding her way around the piles of snow left from clearing the sidewalks, his mother marched across the street straight toward Tea for You.

After looking both ways, he caught up to her at the sidewalk. Putting a hand on her arm, he got her to stop. "Where are we going?"

She tilted up her chin. "Joe is having an open house. I'm showing my support. I am, after all, one of the business owners on this side of town." Josh followed her gaze to Joe, who stood at the door greeting people. Tall and thin, he was dressed in a dark suit, white shirt and lavender tie, and looked better than he had the first time Josh met him. His mom whispered into his ear, "Remind me to tell you how we met. It's a funny story."

When Joe noticed them staring, he smiled and walked out to greet them. "Suzanna, I'm pleased you could grace my humble establishment." He raised her hand to his lips. She wore a silver ring with a ruby on her left hand. Josh recognized his mother's birthstone, a gift from her parents. Her wedding band was well and truly gone.

Josh threw a glance at his mother. She wouldn't put up with the hand-kissing nonsense. But his mother's smile told him otherwise.

Josh glared at the tea shop owner. "You're not from around here, are you?"

"In a roundabout way I am." He pointed to the interior where the Smith brothers stood behind a table pouring small cups of tea. "Hawkeye and Skinny are my uncles."

Taking Josh's mother by the elbow, the tea shop proprietor led her inside.

Josh was left standing alone on the old brick pavers of the carriage house turned library turned tea shop. Kowalsky must have carted the snow around back because the sidewalk was dry and the rosebush-covered fence, which stood between the shop and the new park next door, was free of snow.

A gravel path led to the side of the building. Three wrought-iron tables and chairs graced the small patio. The words Tea for You festooned the upper part of the front door. A cup and saucer with a cookie completed the design he'd spotted before on the big, plate-glass window. The man had done a fine remodeling job.

With a resigned sigh, Josh trailed after his mother into the shop. If his parents stood any chance of reuniting, he had to move fast because clearly Kowalsky was moving plenty fast.

As Josh faced the crowd, he almost turned tail and ran as fast as his legs would take him. He wanted to avoid seeing anybody who might remember him from high school. Yet here he was.

He spied one familiar face he knew he didn't have to worry about. Josh headed toward the table where Hawkeye was busy brewing various teas. Hawkeye had been a fishing buddy of his father's and a man of few words. Perfect. He was almost there when a hand gripped his elbow hard.

"Hey, young fella, have a seat."

Josh jerked to a stop. Hawkeye's brother sat at a small table with an iron teapot on a trivet and two cups and a plate of colorfully decorated treats. "Hello, Mr. Smith. How are you?"

The old farmer waved a hand in the air and motioned again to the chair opposite. "Call me Skinny. Everybody else does."

With a last look at his mother, Josh took the chair. A rich aroma rose from the small teapot. "What are you having?"

"I'm partial to the Rooibos tea, from South Africa, for the powerful antioxidants. I'm a bit sickly, you know. Can I pour you a cup?"

Josh hesitated, but at the hopeful look in the old man's eyes, he nodded. Everyone in town knew Skinny had been sickly as a child, hence the name. Now he wasn't sure if the man was sickly or just accustomed to the idea of being sickly. A flowery fragrance filled his nostrils as he sipped. "Thank you." He looked around the room for his mother, but she had disappeared, as had the tea shop owner. He looked at the clear liquid in the little cup. One gulp, the tea would be gone, and he could make his escape, after a quick hello to Hawkeye.

"Our mother taught us the flavor of food and drink is enhanced when served from nice dishes. We use her wedding china every day." He pointed a long bony finger at the delicate cup in Josh's hand. It was then Josh realized he should have changed clothes. Skinny himself, most often seen in bib overalls and flannel shirts, wore a pair of khaki pants and a pressed brown shirt. Josh looked down at the jeans he had been wearing for three days and the wrinkled shirt with the missing button. He ran a hand over his beard and planned his excuse. "Thanks, Skinny, but—"

"See that young lady over there getting ready to interview my nephew?"

Josh looked, but he couldn't see who

Skinny was referring to for the crowd of people in the shop. "Okay."

"That's the weather girl. Ever since that Atlanta job fell through cuz they figured she wasn't ready for the big time, she's been looking for a story." Skinny rubbed his smooth-shaven chin with thumb and forefinger. "Um-hmm."

"I see." Although he didn't understand what the man was talking about. Eyeing the tiny desserts, Josh figured since he wasn't going anywhere for a moment he might as well try Joe's offerings. They were different from his mother's homemade variety. He chose a small square covered in smooth, blue icing, with a candy flower on top. He wondered if his mother worried about competition. Maybe if he planted the idea in her head, she wouldn't be so attracted to the tea man.

"She asked Hawkeye a few questions about his army days." Skinny chuckled. "But Hawkeye won't talk unless he wants to. She struck out."

The crowd quieted. Josh could see Joe's tall form standing next to the wall of tea in glass jars. A camera was set on a tripod. But, being seated, Josh couldn't see the interviewer. *Sponge cake.* The pretty icing-covered dessert was sponge cake on the inside.

"I'm here at Tea for You in Bear Meadows with proprietor Joe Kowalsky. Tell me, Joe, what brings you to Bear Meadows?"

Josh's ears pricked. He didn't hear Joe's answer, his mind denying what his brain was telling him. He recognized the voice of the interviewer. He stood and stared over the heads of the crowd with disbelief at the young woman next to Joe, microphone in hand. The interviewer was the woman he had rescued from the snowdrift. The woman he had spent the night with in his cabin. The person he had hoped to never see again despite the fact he found her the most intriguing woman he had met in a long time. Wendy. And she looked beautiful. The shiny black hair curled just under her chin. She wore a navy dress with a matching jacket.

He thought she was a teacher. College grad. Living in a small town. She had to be

a teacher. But as he watched her direct her
bright-eyed gaze from the camera lens to
Joe, his heart gradually sank into his toes.

CHAPTER SEVEN

WALT HAD LIKED that first remote broadcast from Little Bear Creek.

His message had been about the open house for the new tea shop in town. Did she want to interview the proprietor? "What happened to Casey doing the interviews?" she'd asked.

"Just never mind and throw in some weather while you're at it," he'd replied.

So here she was, asking the middle-aged man what brought him to Bear Meadows. She had glanced at the camera to make sure the light was on and scanned the crowd when she realized the proprietor hadn't answered. He seemed to have withdrawn. Maybe the crowd had given him stage fright. "Do you have ties to the area?"

His face brightened. "My mother grew up on the farm where my uncles still live. She taught music at Carnegie Mellon University. She's written and recorded a number of songs over her lifetime. She had a beautiful voice."

"Do you sing?" Wendy noticed someone moving at the back of the crowd, but at the same time her reporter's intuition told her there was more to this man than tea.

"Not at all." He stopped for a minute as if uncertain what to say next. Then he brightened. "My mother and I traveled to Asia frequently, and I became interested in teas. We carry over one hundred varieties here. Why don't I show you how to brew loose tea and the differences between brewing herbal, black and green teas? I'll need a few minutes to set things up."

"Sounds intriguing. Thanks, Joe." Wondering how many viewers she could attract to watch a man boil water, she turned back to the camera. "Later we'll show a segment on how to brew the perfect cup of tea." She lowered the microphone and shut off the camera. Her instincts hummed. Something about that interview didn't feel right, and why all the movement in the back of the room?

Gathering up the camera and the tripod, she was trying to be careful so that she didn't bump anybody, when she came face-to-face with the man from the cabin. Her fingers and toes tingled. "Josh." She set the equipment out of the way, avoiding the table with the desserts. "What are you doing here?"

He ran a hand over his blue plaid shirt and appeared decidedly uncomfortable. "I'm not sure. I was visiting my mother at the bakery and somehow I ended up here." He pulled at the threads where he had lost a button. "You must think I really am a mountain man."

Wendy was reminded she had shoved the button in her jeans pocket. She should return it. "Your beard practically guarantees it."

His gaze flicked to the camera. "So, you're a news reporter."

Somehow he made the question sound distasteful, and Wendy got the impression he didn't care much for the profession. Over his shoulder Wendy saw Sue Hunter come out of the back room with Joe. "I think your mom is looking for you." When Josh turned to follow her gaze, Wendy noticed his face hardened as soon as he caught sight of Joe on his mother's heels.

Sue's brow wrinkled as she looked from Wendy to Josh. "Do you two know each other?"

When neither answered, Sue directed her attention to Josh.

Josh answered with a sideways look at Wendy. "I might have saved her life."

Feeling the heat rise into her cheeks, Wendy glanced from Josh to his mother and Joe, staring at her curiously. "You didn't save my life. I would've dug myself out...eventually." Wendy valued her independence. That Josh was convinced she couldn't solve the predicament was irritating.

Josh crossed his arms over his chest and stuck out his chin. "You would have frozen to death."

"No, I wouldn't have." The words came out louder than she intended, causing Cheri from the consignment shop to raise an eyebrow. Cheri was perusing the desserts.

"I see." Sue, wide-eyed and wincing, scanned the room.

Josh cleared his throat. "Mom, Thanksgiving is next week. Are you cooking dinner?"

Sue didn't look at her son, instead she focused on fiddling with the silver buckle at her waist. "I hadn't thought about it." She glanced at Joe.

Josh rocked back on his heels and placed one hand on his mom's arm, as if to draw his mother's attention away from Joe. "Why don't we have dinner at the house, for old times' sake?"

Sue's eyes narrowed but before she could say a word Josh continued. "Dinner for four shouldn't be hard, Mom. I'll help. I mean, you can't cook a holiday dinner at the bakeshop, right?" He glanced at Wendy. "Since your folks are out of town, you might as well come too, Wendy."

She might as well come? What kind of an invitation was that? Both mother and son looked at her expectantly. "Uh, actually…"

But without waiting for Wendy's response, Sue had turned to the tea shop proprietor. "But Joe—"

Wendy had the feeling he wished he had disappeared, as well.

"I'm taking my uncles to a new restaurant in Shadow Falls," Joe explained. He glanced around the room. "If you'll excuse me, it looks like people are leaving. I want to say goodbye." He headed toward the door.

"Great, everyone has somewhere to go." Josh crossed his arms in satisfaction, a habit Wendy was beginning to recognize. He liked to be in control.

Sue watched Joe wend a path through the thinning crowd. "Joe's mother passed away a few months ago. This will be their first Thanksgiving without her. I wanted to—"

"Look, sorry, but I've got to go. I'm not dressed for a tea party." With a glance at Wendy, Josh headed for the back. "See you later."

Wendy wondered if the last comment was directed at his mother or her. "I should take some shots out front before I go. Mrs. Hunter, Josh shouldn't have invited me to Thanksgiving. I—"

"No, it's fine." Sue watched her son as he stopped at one of the tea tables and shook hands with Hawkeye. "If he wants dinner at the house, the least I can do is accommodate him. And I go by Campbell now."

Wendy shook her head. Maybe Josh was right. His family was a lot more complicated than hers. She was about to take the camera outside for those exterior shots when she heard a woman's voice with a sense of urgency. She backed into the space behind the checkout counter and peered between Mrs. Hershberger and Rose Hoffman, who were discussing their teas.

A petite woman in a knee-length, red winter coat was patting Joe on his lavender tie, talking animatedly. The humming started again; Wendy's intuition was on high alert. The woman's facial expression was bright with excitement, not that of someone just coming in for a free cup of tea and a pastry.

Wendy placed the camera on the tripod and positioned it between Mrs. Hershberger and Mrs. Hoffman. Then she turned on the camera. What did she have to lose? She could always delete. She stood on her tiptoes and strained to hear what the woman in the red coat was saying. By now, the commotion had attracted the attention of Rose and Vera.

"I'm looking for Joey Smith. Everyone

used to call him Hawkeye, but I always called him Joey." She pulled off her scarf, revealing a neat cap of soft, white curls. "You must be the nephew, his namesake."

Joe wore the same look he wore when Wendy mentioned his being from Pittsburgh, as if he wanted the conversation to end, or time to go backward. "Yes, ma'am." He threw a worried look toward the back of the room.

She followed Joe's gaze to where Hawkeye stood behind the long table, closing up tea containers and covering the leftover petits fours.

"Joey?" Throwing her coat over the back of a chair, the older woman walked toward him with a big smile. The remaining townspeople backed away, allowing for an open space in the middle of the tearoom. They might have been watching live theater. "Have I finally found you?"

Wendy rotated the camera, following her new star. Her sister used to do this kind of thing all the time, catching people unawares with the camera.

In the middle of tilting a scoop of loose tea leaves into a small bag, Hawkeye glanced up at the sound of the woman's voice. His mouth dropped open. His hazel eyes widened. The tea filled the bag and spilled onto the table.

The woman pressed a manicured hand to her chest. "I've been looking all over for you."

Hawkeye gulped and set the metal scoop on the counter with a clang. "Betty?" His face turned white. His hand clutched his chest. For a minute Wendy feared they would need to call the paramedics. Seeing movement, she glanced at the door leading into the kitchen. Josh hadn't left after all, and he was staring at her with eyes so narrow she couldn't see the blue. She felt a brief disappointment, and then peered into the viewfinder and smiled at what she saw. *Drama, drama, drama.*

"Betty?" Gripping the edge of the table, Hawkeye eased himself onto a stool. "What are you doing here?"

Wendy let out a breath. Color had returned to the older man's face. No paramedics. Skinny, on the other hand, sat stiffly at a nearby table, clearly unhappy.

Silence ensued until Sue approached

Betty, hand outstretched. "I'm Suzanna Campbell. Can I help you?"

Betty accepted Sue's handshake. "My name is Betty. Betty Marino. I used to be Betty Fleck. I grew up in the area."

Sue's eyebrows rose as her blue eyes widened. "You're Betty?"

The woman laughed. "I see you've heard of me." But the laughter faded as she shot Skinny a withering stare. "Not from Jacob, I hope."

"Jacob?" Sue's brow wrinkled just as it had when she came upon Wendy and Josh talking together.

Joe just shook his head. Wendy was enjoying the developing story. She couldn't wait to play it back. The expressions on these faces were priceless.

"I believe the locals know him as Skinny. He was sickly as a child." She turned back to Hawkeye. "Joey, there's someone I want you to meet." She motioned with her hand.

From the crowd emerged a slim young woman with long blond hair. She stopped next to Joe. His words came out in a whisper. "I can't believe it. You look just like—"

"Your mother," Hawkeye said and stared at the girl.

"She's your granddaughter, Joey. Her name is Jessie. And she has a twin brother back in California. I thought the time had come for you to know."

"She's named after my sister?"

Wendy resisted the urge to fist pump. This was good stuff. Wait till Walt saw this footage. And all because she was covering the opening of a little ole tea shop. Then she glanced back at the kitchen. The doorway was empty.

"Well, what do you know about that?" Deb Gold directed her question to Bill the mailman.

"Well, it ain't over, yet." Bill rolled his eyes.

Deb poked him in the ribs. "What are you talking about? And don't say ain't. It's not proper for a civil servant."

"Don't you know? Secrets out in threes. We're not done." The mailman pursed his lips.

Deb leaned in close to her friend and whispered in his ear. "Death comes in threes, not secrets."

Bill shook his head. "No, I'm sure. It's secrets. My grandmother had the second sight, and that's what she used to say. I'm sure of it."

Wendy tightened her fingers around the mike in her hand. She had never heard secrets out in threes. But no matter. If there were two more secrets somewhere in the little burg, she would find them. She started across the room to ask Hawkeye about his love child.

Josh's brainstorm to have a family dinner came after observing the connection between his mother and Joe. Despite his mother's new friendship with the tea shop owner, she was clearly unhappy, as was his father. What better holiday to bring family back together than Thanksgiving, when we're all supposed to be thankful? And Joe was left out. He wasn't sure if he should feel a glimmer of satisfaction about how things had turned out. He didn't feel nearly as good about the spur-of-the-moment invitation to Wendy. He had been on his way out when he heard the commotion. He stayed in the kitchen long enough to hear Hawkeye's granddaughter being introduced. Wow. Talk about secrets. Of all the men Josh knew, Hawkeye was the one he would most want to emulate. He had seemed to have such a handle on the world, so in control of his life. But even he had a secret.

En route to the cabin, Josh stopped by the house. His rumpled attire in the midst of the well-dressed townspeople had reminded him he hadn't showered for a while. The key was still under the third flowerpot to the left, and he let himself into the place, took a quick shower and found some clothes in his room that, miracle of miracles, still fit.

Thirty minutes later he was back driving to the cabin. Despite his dad's offer, he would rather be alone, even if the cabin was cold and uncomfortable. A few coals remained in the fireplace. He was able to add wood. Gradually the cabin heated up. For a few years, he and his parents had come out to the cabin in the summer. They would work on the place together, then his father and he would fish and his mother would read. Then they stopped coming and the cabin was left unfinished. He looked at the pile of stair treads. Nothing said he couldn't do a little work while he was here. He knelt halfway up the stairs, installing the risers and treads.

"About time you came home."

The sunlight lit the lanky form from behind, leaving the face in shadows. But even so, Josh recognized the voice. Hawkeye Smith.

"Hey, you're the last person I expected to see." Josh pounded one last nail. He was almost at the top. Laying down the hammer, he made his way down the stairs. He met Hawkeye in the middle of the room and gripped his hand. The man may be in his seventies, but he had the grip of a twentysomething.

"You disappeared before I had the chance to talk with you." Hawkeye covered both their hands with the other, then released. "I saw the tracks coming to the cabin, so I thought I'd see if it was you. Your parents don't make it out much anymore."

Josh dropped his gaze. "Things got a little crazy."

One corner of the old man's mouth curved upward. "Just a bit." He walked over to the bottom of the stairs. "Finishing the cabin finally? That's good. This is such a prime location."

Many a day Josh had sat with his father and Hawkeye along the bank of the stream. "Still fishing?"

"Not lately." Hawkeye wandered around the room, running a hand over the mantel and admiring the wooden counter in the kitchen. "Your father does nice work."

Josh leaned against the wall, seeing the cabin through Hawkeye's eyes. "He does. Too bad he didn't finish."

Hawkeye took off his ball cap and ran a hand over his bald head before returning the cap to his head. "Is that what you're doing?"

Josh shrugged. "I won't be here long enough, but while I am, I'll do a little."

Hawkeye continued around the room until he came to the foot of the stairs. "One step at a time." He threw Josh a rare smile.

Josh wasn't sure if the man made the pun on purpose or not. "Think there are any trout left in these waters?"

Hawkeye put one foot on the first stair and leaned on his knee. "I wouldn't mind finding out sometime you get the urge to drop a line in the water."

Josh stuck his fingers in the back pockets of his jeans. It was obvious Hawkeye Smith didn't want to talk about the fiasco at the tea shop. The one time Josh had met with a counselor, she had used the term compartmentalize when talking about traumatic events. Josh understood completely. Hawkeye was a private man. He could talk fishing. "I'd have to look around the house. Who knows what my dad did with my gear."

"I can probably come up with an extra rod."

The man just wouldn't give up, but then, Josh wasn't surprised. "Maybe."

"I'll take that as a yes." Hawkeye tapped the bill of his cap with two fingers. "What are you using for railing across the top?"

Josh followed his gaze to the loft area, which extended halfway over the downstairs. "I hadn't got that far."

Hawkeye kept staring up. "There's a place a few miles from here collects pieces from old houses they demolish. We could see if they have any spindles and banisters. Might get lucky."

"Good idea. Thanks." *Not that he would be here.*

A car door slammed, and a moment later Josh heard footsteps on the porch. *What happened to his self-imposed isolation? This place was busier than a fast-food joint at lunchtime on Saturday.* The door flew open.

"Hi. I thought you were here. I brought a picnic." The weather girl stood in the open doorway, a picnic basket in one hand and a bottle of wine in the other. Her mouth dropped open as she caught sight of Josh's other company. "Mr. Smith."

Hawkeye had turned, his back against the wall like an old-time cardplayer. He responded with a slight nod, his expression inscrutable.

Josh wondered what had transpired between the two after he'd left the tea shop. Surely Wendy hadn't tried to turn the woman's announcement into a news story. Then he remembered Skinny's observation. *Ever since the Atlanta job fell through she's been looking for a story.* "I'm surprised to see you here. This place isn't the most comfortable."

Wendy's smile dimmed, but she closed

the door and set the basket and wine on the small table. "I was bored. The Wildflower is closed, and I thought…" Her gaze flicked to the older man still standing like a statue against the wall. "Would you like to join us? I have plenty."

"I was just leaving." Hawkeye raised two fingers to his ball cap, gave a nod to Josh and without another word was gone.

Walking over to the door, Josh watched the older man drive his weathered truck carefully down the road. He had sensed some sort of undercurrent between Wendy and the farmer. *What had she done? Just how desperate was she?* He leaned against the closed door and focused on Wendy shrugging out of her jacket.

How had he missed the station emblem? It was right there, in plain sight.

She unpacked the basket. Wineglasses, plates, cloth napkins, cut-up meats and cheeses. Moving toward the table, he looked down at the bounty and then up until he caught her gaze. "So, you're a news reporter?"

THERE IT WAS AGAIN. The implication that being a news reporter was somehow unworthy. She had seen the guarded look in his eyes when she talked to him at the tea shop. She had gone straight home and emailed all the footage to Walt who, not surprisingly, was at the office on a Sunday afternoon. Her phone rang thirty minutes after she hit the Send button.

"No? Are you kidding me?" Wendy sank into the living-room chair. The black dog studied her from his favorite place on the carpet in front of the fireplace.

"Your assignment was to cover the opening of a tea shop in Bear Meadows and interview the proprietor. What part of that message did you not understand?"

"I did interview the man. After I finished, his old girlfriend from California showed up and announced he had a fifty-year-old daughter and twin grandchildren."

"You sabotaged them, Wendy. This nice old couple who hasn't seen each other for fifty years. And there you are with the camera like a...a paparazzo."

"Thus the story, Walt. Why did Betty marry another man?" She jumped up and

started to pace around the room. The dog's eyes followed her everywhere she went.

"So you want to do entertainment news now?"

"I'm just looking for a story. You used the interview with the little girl during the blizzard."

"A perfect human interest story. A baby being born during a blizzard. Ties in with the weather, too. Your job."

Wendy bit back a groan.

"I might use the tea shop interview for a filler. Look, if this is about your sister..."

"It has nothing to do with my sister." And everything to do with her father's adoration of her sister. The sudden revelation caused her to sit down hard on the couch.

"You do a good job with the weather. Why isn't that enough? The public loves you, and that's why we're keeping you there. So get used to it."

An hour later Wendy still steamed over Walt's rejection of her footage. The dog had finally risen from his spot and now rested his chin on her knee. "What do you think I should do?"

And now here she was. Because if she

had stayed home she would have thought about the rejection all night. Also, she had nowhere else to go.

She chose to ignore Josh's question for the moment. "Are you hungry?" Opening the wine, she poured them each a glass. "Not knowing the type of wine you prefer, I brought a merlot and some cheddar." She handed Josh a glass. "Cheers."

Josh accepted the glass. "Cheers." But instead of sitting down, he continued to walk around the room, his head down as if he were thinking heavy thoughts.

Taking her glass, she went over to the fireplace. Encountering Hawkeye when she opened the cabin door had completely thrown her for a loop. She had only made it halfway across the tea shop, microphone in hand, when the older man shot a warning look in her direction. Hawkeye was the kind of man who preferred to stay in the shadows. He wouldn't take kindly to camera lights. And watching Josh here, she realized he was a younger version of the reclusive farmer. They both played their cards close to the vest. "Maybe I shouldn't have come. I interrupted your work."

Josh stopped at the base of the stairs. "You don't like asking for help, do you?"

"What are you talking about?"

"When I said I saved your life. I was just teasing. But your face…you had this expression…" Josh joined her in front of the fire. A log dropped, scattering sparks.

Wendy sipped the wine, welcoming the brief fizz on her tongue and the warmth sliding down her throat. Josh had hit the nail on the head. The revelation she had earlier, of how her father continuously praised her older sister's accomplishments, had caused her to question her goals. But he and Hawkeye weren't the only ones who didn't want to talk about personal issues.

"Maybe we should put this away." Finishing his wine, Josh set the glass on the table with a quiet thump.

Instead, Wendy picked up the bottle and started to refill his glass. Before she could, Josh placed his hand, palm down, over the top of the glass. She looked up and caught his gaze. "The party's just getting started."

Taking the bottle from her hand, Josh set the wine on the table. He pulled her toward him. "You're a complicated woman,

Wendy Valentine. I don't have room in my life for complications."

She wanted to resist. She really did. *No men, no kids, not even a pet.* The dog currently in her house had a home somewhere else, she was sure of it. And the man who had his arms around her and smelled of sandalwood and spice with a hint of wood smoke was leaning in for a kiss. He belonged somewhere, too…just not with her. Still, it didn't stop her from kissing him back.

CHAPTER EIGHT

SHE ARRIVED PROMPTLY at noon. They were eating at two. When Josh opened the door, the sight of her almost took his breath away. Her dark hair, as always, swung in a smooth line that ended just under her chin. She wore ivory wool slacks, a matching turtleneck sweater and a navy blue pea-coat. The red scarf added a pop of color. She stood there expectantly, and Josh realized she was waiting to be invited into the house. He stood back. "You look…nice."

He hadn't seen her since Sunday evening, when they had ended up enjoying the food and the fire, and kissing again before Wendy said she had to go. The intensity of his feelings for her had frightened him.

She shrugged as she passed him. "Thank you, but you've been looking at cows all summer so…" The smile she threw at him almost knocked him back. Shutting the door, he paused, wondering what had possessed him to invite her for a family holiday dinner. Then he remembered his goal. Right, reuniting his parents. Wendy was here as a buffer. She lifted her chin as she sniffed. "The turkey smells great. I'm not surprised, since your mom is cooking."

"Can I take your coat?"

She set a bottle of wine on the hall table and swirled so he could pull the coat from her shoulders. Her floral scent enveloped him, and he shut his eyes for a moment. "Mom's in the kitchen. We got here at ten." He led her down the hallway, passing the archway into the almost empty living room. His mother had yet to comment on the disappearance of her furniture. Josh had returned his grandmother's rocking chair, thinking the room wouldn't look so bare. But it did.

"Hello, Wendy." Josh's mother didn't look up as she stirred a thick white dressing into shredded cabbage.

The kitchen was warm and filled with the scent of roasting turkey. Steam bubbled from a pan on the stove, filming the window over the kitchen sink with fog. Wendy glanced at Josh and then back at his mother. "I brought wine. You're such a good cook I figured you had everything else."

"Wine is fine. I'm sure we'll need it before the day is over." His mom dropped the empty container in the sink and acted as if she were on the job, instead of preparing a meal for her loved ones.

"What can I do to help?"

"The glasses are probably dusty. If you want to check them, maybe wipe them out. You can set the table."

"What about me, Mom?"

His mother looked him up and down. "Well, son, you could clean up a bit."

Josh ran a hand over his beard. "Okay." He was glad to leave the kitchen. Four days since he and Wendy had cozied up in front of the fire in the cabin, and he thought he finally had his feelings under control. But when he saw her on the porch, he was unprepared for the longing he felt. He needed to get a handle on his feelings. Heck, he needed to get a handle on his life. Ever since he had seen that picture of his mother, things had been tumbling out of place.

In what was once his childhood bedroom, he looked in his closet. His baseball trophies sat on the top shelf along with his high school yearbooks. The clothes he had worn to church Easter Sunday with his mother over three years ago still hung in the closet. If he hurried, he'd still have plenty of time to spend in the company of the lovely weather reporter.

WENDY HADN'T SPENT much time with the bakeshop owner. The few times she had encountered Mrs. Hunter in The Wildflower the woman had been brusque. Today, in the home she used to share with the man who cheated on her, she didn't seem much friendlier.

"Just four of us, right?" Wendy propped her hands on her hips and tried to figure out where the glasses would be stored.

"Um-hmm."

Wendy opened four cupboard doors before she found matching water and wineglasses. Opening a drawer under the counter, she lucked out on the first try and found a tea towel. "Mrs. Hunter, do you know—"

"Remember? I go by Campbell these

days, Wendy, but you can call me Sue. Everybody else does." She transferred the coleslaw to a crystal bowl and placed it in the refrigerator. "Except Joe." Hands in the dishwater, she stood by the sink, staring out the window. "He calls me Suzanna."

The woman was in her own home, with her husband and son, but she seemed conflicted, that much was certain. "You must be glad to have Josh home." Wendy held a glass up to the light. Definitely dusty. She wiped out the interior of the glass and hazarded a look at her hostess.

A smile lit the woman's face as she resumed washing the dishes. "I've missed him." She was quiet a minute. "I'll do anything to spend time with my son, even spend a day in this house sharing a meal with his father."

Wendy eyed the stack of paper plates in one corner of the counter and the half-empty potato chip bag on top of the refrigerator. "You can tell a woman doesn't live here."

"Anymore." Sue stressed the last half of the word as she rinsed and dried the dish with a towel. "The dishes in the china cabinet need a swipe with the cloth, too."

Wendy had glanced into the dining room as she'd followed Josh down the hall. The only thing on the dining-room table was a stack of newspapers. "Shall I set the table?"

Sue nodded. "There should be a tablecloth in one of the drawers." She muttered under her breath. "Should be."

Relieved to escape the tension, Wendy spent the next few minutes getting the table ready for their dinner. She found long white tapers and a set of crystal candleholders and put them in the center of the table, which she had covered with a green cloth. Finally, she could think of nothing more to add and carried the stack of newspapers into the kitchen where she put them next to the chip bag. "I love your dishes."

"My mother's wedding china. I should pack up the dishes and take them home. Heaven knows Brad won't need them." She opened the oven door and removed the turkey and set it on the stove. Then she placed a tray of rolls in the oven. "But then, I don't have a home. Almost ready."

"The turkey smells terrific." Wendy had

to admit she was starved for some home-made food. Since her parents had left she had existed on yogurt and cereal. She caught a glimpse of her hostess's face as she set the timer. She had watched as the woman's weight had steadily dropped in the last year. Her deteriorating marriage must have taken away her appetite. "So you don't see yourself moving back in?"

"Are you kidding?"

Wendy knew she was digging where it was none of her business, but sometimes she just couldn't help herself. And she wanted to understand Josh's need to leave home so quickly. "Things must have been different when Josh was still around."

Sue propped a hip against the sink and finally gave Wendy her full attention. "When he was little, things were different. We were both busy working, Josh was into sports. But somewhere along the way, things started to go downhill. Brad and I disagreed when Josh should head off to college. Brad wanted him to help with the landscaping business, and I thought he should begin school summer semester. Even then I was thinking of early retirement so I could start the bakery. But I planned to stay at the university long enough for Josh to get his degree. He had reduced tuition because I was a secretary in the chemistry department." She raised her brows. "Brad never wanted me to open my own business."

"Why didn't Josh go to college?"

"He did. He was taking biology at Penn State with plans of becoming a physical therapist. He and Dr. Reed used to talk about anatomy all the time. That and sports fascinated Josh from the beginning. Josh played ball in high school."

"Dr. Reed?"

"Deb Gold's father. Brad had the contract for the grounds at the mansion Josh's senior year of high school. He was so busy Josh ended up doing most of the work. Which is why we argued about when Josh would start school. I'm sure Josh felt guilty leaving his father without help that summer."

"Smells good in here. It smells like home."

At the sound of Josh's voice, Wendy turned and dropped the stemmed wineglass in her hand. "Oh my." Josh grabbed it before it hit the floor.

He smiled at Wendy's surprise. "I look that different?"

"Oh my." For a woman who made her living with words, she was having a hard time thinking of anything other than *oh my*. The beard had hidden his strong features. His father's strong, defined jaw, and his mother's telling smile.

"There's my boy." Sue reached up and rested her palm on Josh's cheek. "I knew somewhere behind that scruffy beard was my handsome son."

"This face is better off hidden, Mom." He ran a hand over his hair, which he had combed back from his face, but it was still long enough to touch the collar of the navy blue pullover he wore with dark jeans.

Sue stood on tiptoes and gave her son a quick kiss. "You look *much* better." She turned back to the stove. "Whew. I thought you were going to keep that look forever."

Wendy remained frozen, gripping the edge of the counter with one hand and the towel with the other. She wouldn't have minded kissing that smooth-shaven man herself, except that wasn't what they were about. *She was here because...because...*

"You might want to tell your father dinner will be on the table in five minutes." Sue was peeking at the rolls in the oven.

"I'll carry the turkey in," she offered.

Five minutes later Wendy sat down to dinner with the Hunters. The golden turkey sat on a flowered meat platter in front of Brad, where he stood holding a wide knife, prepared to carve the turkey. Mashed potatoes, sweet potato casserole, corn, a basket of Sue's perfectly browned rolls completed the meal.

"This smells delicious, Sue." Brad Hunter sent his wife a slight smile.

His mother gave a slight headshake. "Wendy, would you like a roll?"

Wendy nodded. *No prayer before the meal? No what am I thankful for? Just pass the rolls.*

Mr. Hunter persevered. "The turkey looks good, Sue. Small, but good."

"With only four people we didn't need a twenty-pound bird, Brad." Sue fluffed out her cloth napkin and slid it over her lap. "What is your family doing today,

Wendy?" She handed her a bowl of mashed potatoes.

Wendy accepted the bowl and spooned a portion onto her plate. "They're visiting my sister in New York City. I think they went out to eat."

"I'll bet that's expensive. Thanksgiving dinner in New York City. Hold up your plate, Wendy." Mr. Hunter forked a long slice of turkey onto her plate.

"Sounds like fun to me. It would be nice for once not to have to do all the work for a holiday meal." Sue glared at her husband down the length of the table. She held out her plate.

Brad put turkey on her plate. "Maybe someday you'll have a daughter-in-law who can cook."

Sue's eyes narrowed. "You know men can—"

"We forgot the coleslaw." Josh jumped out of his seat. "I'll get it, Mom."

"And I'll get the wine." Still in shock over Josh's transformation, she had completely forgotten the bottle of wine she'd brought. She followed him into the kitchen. She suspected Josh was as anxious to escape the tension in the room as she. With his back to her, he stood staring at the contents of the refrigerator.

"Coleslaw."

He nodded. "Thanks. It'd slipped my mind."

"Easy to do." She opened the wine and caught him studying her. "What?"

"Are you sorry you came?"

"Are you kidding?" She cupped his face and marveled at the smooth-shaven jaw. "I would've shown up for bologna sandwiches just to see you cleaned up."

He kissed her then, so quickly he was out of the room before she knew what had happened.

Right. Back to the dining room, she thought. "Here you go. White wine to accompany the turkey." She smiled at the solemn family and wondered how many times in the past Josh had acted as intermediary for his parents.

"Where have you been staying, Josh?" his father asked. "I left the light on the night you stopped here, but I guess you found somewhere else to sleep."

Wendy caught Mr. Hunter's raised eyebrow. She waited for Josh to correct his father's erroneous assumption. When he didn't respond. She did. "You've been staying at the cabin, right?"

"I've been hungry for halupki. Any plans to make some, Mom?"

"I usually make it for Christmas." She looked at him. "Will you still be home? Or do you have to be back on base?" Sue's brow wrinkled in thought. "But then, come to think of it, how did you grow such a long beard? Were you on special assignment?"

Wendy looked at Josh in surprise. *Back on base?* She thought he was working on a ranch somewhere. Then she remembered the *oh dark thirty* reference.

"You've been on leave, haven't you, son?" Mr. Hunter poured gravy from a flowered pitcher and offered the dish to Wendy.

She shook her head.

Brad set the pitcher back on the matching saucer. "Living it up, eh? Where'd you go? Some tropical island?"

Josh looked decidedly uncomfortable. He glanced at her but quickly looked away. "I'm out." He said the words so quietly everyone else at the table stopped what they were doing.

"You're what?" Mr. Hunter's dark eyebrows drew together.

Josh finished his wine in one gulp. "I said, I'm out."

The only sound was the clanking of silverware as his parents resumed eating as if uncertain how to respond.

"Well, I for one am glad that we'll see more of you." His mother's face lit with a rare smile.

Setting down his fork, Mr. Hunter leaned back in his chair and favored his son with a steady look. "You'll be needing work. I don't have much going on right now, but if you're still around by summer, you can help me."

His parents had spoken at the same time and then stared at each other. Sue finally broke the silence. "Don't start that again."

"Why not? He's a grown man. He has to have a job."

"He can go back to school." Sue's face lit up. "Can you use the GI Bill? You can live here and go to Penn State, just like we planned."

"I'm not sticking around." Now that the beard was gone, Josh's expression was easier to read. His face reddened as his parents discussed his future.

Maybe it was her turn to change the subject. Seeing Josh's empty glass, she reached for the wine bottle. "More wine?"

Just as he had at the cabin, Josh rested the palm of his hand over the empty glass. "No, thanks." He gave her a polite smile.

One glass. Again he had one glass of wine. "Your mom said you went to Penn State for a semester." As soon as she said the words, she knew she'd said the wrong thing. But then, conversation with these three was a veritable minefield. "We would've been there at the same time."

"I was just there summer semester."

"Oh. I didn't start until fall."

"I flunked out. Not college material."

"Nonsense. You were honors list in high school. You could've been a doctor."

"If he'd stayed home that summer and helped me with the business, he wouldn't have gone out and partied so much. That's why he flunked out. Drinking."

Wendy waited for Josh to defuse the

escalating fight but he seemed lost, staring at his plate of food in deep thought. "Well, high school to college is certainly an adjustment, I can tell you." She tried to catch someone's eye, but each member of the family seemed engrossed in the meal. "I was worried a few times."

Slamming down her fork, Sue raised her head and stared at who Wendy figured was the woman's soon to be ex-husband. "By the way, what happened to the living-room furniture? I want it back."

"As soon as these dishes are done, I'm leaving. And if I had anywhere to put the entire set, I'd take the china with me." Sue turned from the sink and caught her son's gaze. "Maybe I could put them in the basement of the tea shop. Temporarily."

"Mom, settle down. Dad's sorry."

"He's sorry no one is here to cook and clean for him, that's all he's sorry about." She scrubbed at the bottom of the roasting pan, her face red with effort. Josh stopped her and took over scrubbing. "You know how he is when he thinks he's right, Josh."

Of course he did. Josh had seen that

look of resolution on his father's face many times. He knew no amount of persuasion or promises would convince his father to change his mind.

"Please, Dad. Can I have the car to-night? I promise I'll be home by midnight."

"No. I might need it and besides, I don't think you should be gallivanting around the countryside."

So he had biked to Dr. Reed's and let himself into the big mansion. Dr. Reed was at a medical school reunion in Philadelphia. He had the house to himself. He wandered around until he found himself in the study, the room where he and Dr. Reed discussed sports, anatomy and sometimes even girls. Dr. Reed had fallen in love with his wife when they were twelve, and he had found no one to replace her since she passed away ten years earlier. The whiskey sat on a silver tray in a crystal decanter. Dr. Reed's one indulgence. That and the car. But he liked one or two glasses of the high-end whiskey after dinner a couple of nights a week. He called them highballs.

Josh carried a stack of plates into the dining room and put them away. He could hear his father's voice from the living room. He entered the hallway and moved to the archway of the living room. Wendy sat in the rocking chair and his father in the recliner.

"You can keep that."

Wendy stuffed a sheaf of papers into her large handbag. Seeing Josh in the doorway, she stood. "I should go. Thank you for your hospitality, Mr. Hunter."

Josh shook his head. His father had done none of the food preparation. But he seemed to have taken a shine to Wendy. "You're welcome, young lady. Glad you could join us."

"I'll walk you out." Sue stood next to him in the archway, her lips pressed tight. She thrust her arms into her coat sleeves. "I'll be taking my dishes, Brad."

"Are you sure you don't want to leave them here awhile? Maybe we'll have Christmas dinner together." His dad shot a look at him as if pleading with him to agree and encourage his mother to celebrate another holiday at the house.

"Could I have my coat?" Wendy was standing in front of him, her face expressionless.

"Sure." Retrieving her coat from the hall closet, Josh held it out as she slipped her arms into the sleeves. Again the floral scent as she moved close. She turned to face him. Behind him Josh could feel his mother's presence as she waited at the front door. Putting her hands on his shoulders, Wendy stood on her tiptoes and kissed his cheek. "I can't say I miss the beard." She smiled and disappeared out the door with his mother. He waited until both women had driven away and returned to the living room, where he settled into the rocking chair vacated by Wendy. He could still feel her warmth in the faded print cushion, flattened by generations of Hunter behinds.

Feet propped up, his father sat in the recliner watching a football game on the giant-screen television. "With your mother starting that fight, we didn't get any dessert. Wonder if she left the pumpkin pie?"

Josh stared at his father, whose attention was still on the screen. For the first time he wondered if his father really loved his mother, or if he just wanted things to go back to the way they were so he could be comfortable. Josh leaned forward, elbows on knees, hands clasped, and stared at the beige carpet that his mother had installed the summer before his senior year. From the marks left by the missing furniture, he could see the carpet hadn't been shampooed in a long time.

"Why don't you stay in your old room? That cabin must be freezing."

Josh glanced at the screen. Halftime. His father's attention was once again on him. "I'm not staying, Dad."

"I don't know what's going on with you. Does that pretty weather girl have something to do with it? You afraid of falling for her? She's got her eyes on the bright lights of the big city, you know. If you're looking for a girlfriend, you should go to the library."

"Why would I go to the library for a girlfriend?"

"The new librarian. Eliza." His eyes wide, Brad gestured at Josh. "Nice girl. She opened a cat rescue at her home. You could do worse."

"I never knew you to visit the library, Dad."

"Yeah, well." He settled back into his chair and focused on the commercials.

"Remember that night I asked for the car and you said no?" He had to tell someone. Being in this town, knowing what he had done, was eating him up inside. Hawkeye's secret had emerged after fifty years. Is that what he had to look forward to? The threat of his secret always being found out?

His father's dark eyebrows knit together. "Seems to me there were lots of nights you asked for the car and I said no. We couldn't afford repairs if you had an accident. I'm getting pie." He put down the footrest with a thump and disappeared into the kitchen. He came back with a saucer of pumpkin pie with whipped topping and a cup of coffee. "I left the pie on the counter for you." He sat in his chair, set the coffee on the table next to the chair and concentrated on the game.

Josh continued to stare at the beige carpet. All he really wanted to do was follow Wendy out the door. He should be able to tell his dad. Something like this was exactly what a father was for. Now he had his doubts.

At the next commercial his dad looked over at him. "When you said you're not staying, did you mean here at the house, or did you mean in Bear Meadows?"

"I can't stay here, Dad. That's what I'm trying to tell you. I can't stay *here*."

"You hate this town?"

Josh shook his head. If he could only get the words out, his father would understand. "I don't hate this town."

"Oh, I get it." Brad picked up his coffee and took a sip. "You don't hate Bear Meadows." He set down the cup and threw his son a grim smile. "You just hate your father."

CHAPTER NINE

THE DOG GREETED her as soon as she unlocked the door. He seemed to understand her feeling of melancholy instantly. She let him out into the yard and sat on the porch while he sniffed spots on the ground and near the trees. The blue jay was back.

"Come on, bird, you must have a story I can use." She rocked gently and watched the dog, wondering what was keeping him here, wondering why he didn't go home. She would have to take him to the pound. Although, at this rate, it didn't seem as if she were going anywhere. She would be on WSHF reporting the forecast for the rest of her life.

The temperature dropped with the setting of the sun. When the dog came back to her, they both went inside. She changed out of her clothes into a pair of yoga pants and a loose sweatshirt.

She curled up in a comfy chair in front of the fireplace and turned on the television, flipping channels until she found a rerun of the morning's parade. The book in her lap was open to the same page it had been ten minutes ago. Somehow she couldn't read, which was unusual for her. She checked her phone for messages. None. Well, nothing said she couldn't call them, right?

She had no sooner picked up her phone than it rang. Expecting the caller to be her mother, she didn't even look at the display when she answered. "I was just about to call you."

"Really?"

Wendy recognized the Southern lilt, but she still looked at the display. *Katherine King.* The headhunter. Her heart beat a little faster. "I thought my mom was calling, Ms. King. I'm surprised to hear from you. Did you have a nice holiday?"

"Very nice and I'm sorry to bother you. I hope I'm not catching you at a bad time?" Her sweet-sounding lilt made Wendy feel as if they were having tea in the drawing room of a Southern mansion.

Wendy glanced down at the sleeping

dog. *This is it, Rover. My big chance.* "No, go ahead."

"A small affiliate station in Miami is looking for a morning news anchor. I know it's not exactly investigative journalism of the first order, but at least you would get more experience than doing the weather. Are you interested?"

As quickly as Wendy's hopes had risen, they fell. Another small station. "Can I think about it?"

"Of course. But they're filling the position after the first of the year."

"Déjà vu." Almost a year ago Wendy had been preparing to leave for Atlanta. What a mess that had turned into.

"Exactly, well, get back to me as soon as you can. Y'all have a nice day, honey."

She decided to call her mother, who didn't answer, but then, she didn't believe in carrying a phone everyplace she went. Neither did her father. Maybe it was a generational thing.

"What have you done with our parents?" Wendy finally called and asked her sister, surprised that she actually answered.

"Dad wanted to go to a cigar bar." Katie

Valentine yawned. "Thank goodness, because that lets me out and I'm exhausted. They have much more energy since they've retired."

"And Mom went along? Where's Oliver?" Wendy knew her sister had a busy work schedule. She could only imagine the extra demands her parents had placed on her sister's time.

"Dad went to the botanical gardens with her, so I'm guessing it was part of a negotiated deal." Her velvet-toned voice dripped with irony. "And I'm the designated dog sitter."

Wendy laughed. They shared only one parent, but Katie had been thirteen when the two married. Despite the age difference, the two sisters often had a real fondness for each other, usually at their parents' expense. "Am I interrupting your work?"

"It's Thanksgiving, little sister."

"That never stopped you before."

"I'm in between jobs right now. I'm watching a rerun of the parade and having a glass of wine."

"Me, too." Wendy glanced over at the television where horses with their riders pranced down the street. She was about to ask how her sister managed to be in between jobs when her sister continued.

"I wish you were here. Why didn't you come along?"

"Work. Why else?" The dog chose that moment to look over his shoulder as if to say, *and you had to take care of me.*

"You don't have to tell me. Although you could've come up for the day. What have you been up to?"

"I went out."

"Good. I imagine the local restaurants had the traditional meal."

"Hmm, I was invited to the home of a friend."

"Really. A girlfriend?"

"No."

"A boyfriend? I can't believe my ears. I thought you had sworn off men."

"He kind of rescued me during the blizzard, so I felt, um, obligated. But he's not a boyfriend, just a friend."

"Sounds like he has potential to me." Her voice was teasing.

Wendy didn't remember her famous sister ever teasing about relationships. Up until the last year, every conversation had centered on her job or her next assignment. "Listen, I need some advice."

"On men? I'm the last one to give advice. I haven't had a date in years." A sigh sounded over the phone.

"No. On work. The station manager suggested I interview the owner of a tea shop that opened in town. Just a regular boring old interview. And then in walks this woman and she proceeds to tell the owner's uncle, who is in his seventies, former military and kind of mysterious, that he has a daughter and twin grandchildren out in California. I mean, he's just found this out."

"Wow. Interesting story." Katie sounded intrigued.

"That's what I thought. But Walt said no." Wendy drummed her fingers on the arm of the chair.

"He had to. They're private citizens, Wendy. They're entitled to their privacy." Her voice was matter-of-fact.

"But my story, as it stands, is boring."

"Does your tea shop owner have a criminal record?" Katie's voice sharpened.

Wendy thought of the wrinkled newspaper Josh's father had given her. "Maybe."

Katie didn't respond at first, as if thinking through the possibilities. "There you go. Hey, Mom and Dad just came back. Do you want to talk to them?"

She was about to say yes when the dog's ears pricked just before the doorbell sounded. "Someone's here. Give them my love." She didn't have a chance to mention the Miami offer, but then, Katie probably wouldn't have been impressed.

Her sister laughed. "Go for the jugular. Find his vulnerable spot. Then you've got yourself an interview. Good luck, honey."

The dog was already looking up at the knob of the kitchen door when she arrived. "I don't trust you, fella. You'd let in a burglar if he scratched your belly." Although the sun had set, there was enough light that she could peek out the window to see who stood on the back porch.

She opened the door, unable to contain her smile.

Josh held up a golden crust pie in the palms of both hands like an offering. "You missed dessert."

WENDY MADE COFFEE, and they each ate two slices of apple pie in the kitchen, the second accompanied with a scoop of vanilla ice cream. "I'm surprised your dad allowed you out of the house with this."

"He doesn't know." Josh grinned. He had been prepared to tell his father the whole story, when the man had suddenly shut down, convinced he was the reason Josh was leaving Bear Meadows. But the fact was, after his father's comment, Josh saw the pie on the counter, and the only thing he could think about was Wendy and so he had driven here, as if on autopilot. "Don't feel too badly. He ate half of the pumpkin."

Josh felt a nudge at his knee. Reaching down, he ran a hand over the top of the dog's smooth dome. "Did you name this guy yet?"

"Rover seems appropriate. At least for now." She carried their plates over to the sink. "I just got a call from my headhunter. A station in Miami is looking for a morning anchor. It's an affiliate, small, but I would get some news experience."

Josh's heart flipped in his chest. He drummed his fingers on the table, taking a moment to remind himself this was as it was meant to be. He had to admit though, he was becoming attached to the young woman with the dark eyes. "No risk of being caught in a blizzard."

She slammed shut the door of the dishwasher. "Just hurricanes. Hey, want to come into the den? It's more comfortable." She held out a hand.

Josh looked at the slim unadorned hand, then took it in his and followed her down the hallway. He stopped at a photograph with a familiar face. "Who's this?" He recognized Wendy in the picture, but next to her was someone else he thought he knew. The two women looked similar except for the hair. Wendy's was a dark brown shade, the other woman's hair was honey blond.

"You don't know?"

Josh peered at Wendy, who had a funny look on her face. "She looks familiar."

"She should. She interviews the rich and famous, world leaders, covers everything from foreign affairs to awards ceremonies. She's—"

"Katie Valentine is your sister?" Josh turned back to the photo, recognition suddenly dawning. Of course, this woman had been on national news for years. He suddenly felt queasy at the thought he was becoming friends with her sister. He also understood Wendy's need to move up in her professional world. She was probably being constantly compared to her successful, older sister.

"Yep." Wendy pulled him into the den, where a fire burned in the fireplace and a book lay facedown in the chair next to it. The parade still played on the television.

"You built a fire?"

"It's gas. I flip a switch. My parents are all about convenience." She grabbed a throw and two pillows off the couch and tossed them on the floor in front of the fire. "Have a seat and I'll get some wine." She turned off the television.

Josh settled himself on the floor and leaned back against the couch. Now that he was closer he could see that the fireplace was gas. The dog curled up on the hearth. Josh leaned over and whispered into his ear. "I wouldn't get too comfortable, Rover. It's only a matter of time before she moves on."

The dog propped his head on his paws and stared at Josh, his brows wrinkled as if he, too, were concerned.

Wendy returned with a glass in each hand. "I'm glad you came by. I felt kind of bad leaving so quickly."

"My parents are known for throwing ice water on a party." Josh accepted his glass and tried not to react as Wendy settled next to him and drew the throw over their legs. It was too cozy for comfort. "Did you talk to yours today?"

"I called, but they were out doing their own thing." Her words had a melancholy sound. She sipped her wine. "I talked to my sister."

"You did? The famous Katie? She wasn't flying somewhere to interview an important person?"

"I did. And I had assumed the same. She might be reevaluating things. She sounded a bit weird."

He put his arm around her shoulders and tugged on a strand of hair. "So you want to follow in your sister's footsteps. You want to be famous."

"I just want—" she ran a finger over the

rim of the glass "—I don't know. A big story, I guess. Something that matters, that interests people."

She was quiet a minute, her gaze on the flames. "Do you think that's wrong?"

"Only you have the answer to that." Josh ran a strand of her dark hair through his fingers, savoring the soft silkiness.

"And what about you?"

"What about me?" Josh's gut clenched.

"Why didn't you tell me you were in the army?"

"Because I'm out. It's in the past."

"Your mom said you were planning on being a physical therapist."

He shrugged, wishing his mother hadn't said as much.

"She said you worked for Dr. Reed."

"Dr. Reed was a client of my dad's."

"She said you were close, that you would talk medicine."

"Yep. He was a cool guy, a good man." He thought of the tall, white-haired gentleman with the steady hands and long tapered fingers. Capable of delivering a baby or loosening the nut under an oil pan.

"You could go back to school."

He leaned his head on the couch cushion and shut his eyes. He was tired of thinking about the future, and he was tired of thinking about the past. "I'm too old."

Wendy laughed. "You're not old." She slipped her hand into his. "You know, we just missed each other at Penn State."

He kept his eyes closed and focused on the feel of her soft hand as her fingers tightened. "Hmm?"

"You were on campus summer semester and I was there fall. We just missed each other."

Josh opened his eyes and found her studying his face. He lifted a hand and ran a finger over her cheek. "Honey, you wouldn't have liked me back then."

"That's the third time today I've been called honey." She smiled. "So you partied a lot. Did you have a beard?"

"No." So much else was different then, too. The summer after the incident his head hadn't been his own. At one point, he thought he might lose his mind and had made an appointment with a school counselor, only to cancel at the last minute. When Wendy pressed against his chest, he rested his chin on top of her head. He was staring into the fire as she asked her next question.

She twisted in his arms and gave him a curious look. "Do you know Deb Gold?"

He took a deep breath before he answered. "Deb was a real estate agent when I was in school. She was a widow, but she didn't live at the mansion."

"Did you know she's selling her father's classic car?"

He didn't move, but his body tensed at the mention of the car. "No."

"Did you ever drive it?"

Josh felt a strange sensation of something crawling on his skin. Wendy was smart. It was only a matter of time before she was at a major station. She had that ability to work at a knot until she unraveled it.

"She's thinking of selling the mansion, too. I'd love to see the inside." She smiled. "You must have been inside."

Josh nodded.

"Hey, your glass is empty." She jumped up and retrieved the bottle from a side table that looked like an antique. She was about to refill his glass, but Josh put his palm on the rim. "No, thanks."

She leaned back on her heels and fixed him with a pensive stare. "Just one glass, huh?"

Josh nodded and looked away. "Just one."

She returned the bottle to the table and sat down again.

"Why are you so anxious to leave home? You've traveled. I haven't. I can't go until I land that job. But what are you looking for?"

Josh looked at the flames. What, indeed?

Josh made himself a highball and settled into Dr. Reed's chair. Maybe someday he would have a house like this, a successful physical therapy practice, and would sit, at the end of the day, and have a highball. He coughed at the first swallow, but by the time the glass was empty, he felt a warm glow. His father treated him like a child. Dr. Reed spoke to him as an equal. In fact, they had taken the car out for a drive one sunny Saturday afternoon, and Dr. Reed had allowed Josh to drive it back home. If Dr. Reed were his father, he would have al-

lowed Josh to take the car for the evening.
He poured another drink.

"Or are you running away?"

The words came as if from a distance. Josh tore his gaze from the blue flames and stared into beautiful brown eyes he could get lost in. "Excuse me?"

She propped herself on her hip so she could look directly into his face. "You can't bear to see your parents fighting, so you're running away."

He placed his palm on her cheek and ran his thumb along her chin. "Always thinking. I don't want to talk about the past, and I don't want to talk about the future. Why don't we just stay in the moment, Miss Valentine?" And with that he pulled her into his arms and kissed her.

Thanksgiving night, a fire in the fireplace, alone in the big house. This was all he wanted for now. Because once Miss Wendy Valentine found out the truth about him, there would be no more kisses. Once Miss Wendy Valentine found out he had run away after almost killing a man, she would have her big story and she would be on her way.

CHAPTER TEN

MARK HAD TAKEN another long weekend to ski in Vermont, so Wendy was prepared to stay late on Friday as she drove to the station in Shadow Falls. After a series of forty-degree days, the snow from the blizzard was almost gone and the highway was dry. Thankfully. The first person she saw was Casey. He crooked a finger when he saw her come into the studio.

"What's up?" Grabbing a coffee from the beverage station, she sat on the adjacent stool and waved to a cameraman. Josh had stayed late the night before. He had stopped at one glass of wine, but she didn't, and her head felt as if a fog had moved in for the duration. She took a long swallow of black coffee. She needed all the caffeine she could get.

"I wanted to ask you something." He winked.

She groaned. Maybe he was going to ask her out. "I've got to go to my office."

"Wait. I need your opinion. I met someone." He reached in his pocket and then placed a small black velvet box in Wendy's palm. "Take a look and tell me what you think."

Wendy almost choked on her coffee. "You met someone? I didn't even know you were dating." Setting down her cup, she flipped open the lid of the box. Nestled inside was a princess cut diamond ring. She brought it close to better inspect the jewelry. "Oh my goodness, Casey. This is gorgeous." She glanced up at her coworker. He hadn't been flirting with her at all.

Casey winked, a satisfied smile on his face. "Uh-huh. She's an optometrist. I saw her for my first appointment."

"How romantic." Wendy closed the lid and handed the box back to Casey. "I have to ask you something."

"Two minutes." The voice of the intern came over the loudspeaker. Wendy noted idly that her squeaky voice had disappeared.

"Make it quick." Casey stuck the box in

his pocket and turned to gather his notes from the anchor desk.

"If you're asking this woman to marry you, how did you know she was the one?"

Casey looked up in shock. "What do you mean how? You just know. There's an awareness. A spark. And then everything flows easily from there. Becky's my soul mate."

"Soul mate? That sounds so...final."

Casey's face flushed. "Excuse me?"

Wendy hid her cup under the counter and walked over to the weather board. Casey was a few years older than she, and Wendy had assumed he was looking for greener professional pastures, as well. But maybe he had already found them. Miami was looking better and better.

At the completion of the broadcast, she stopped at Walt's office. Still surprised at Casey's announcement, she didn't tell Walt about the Miami job. Nor did she mention the information from Brad Hunter. She hadn't figured out quite yet what to do about it.

Walt lounged in his desk chair and waited for Wendy to take a seat, which she couldn't do until she removed the stack of newspapers from the only chair. She noticed the box of photographs in the same spot as before. "Still mad at me?"

Wendy jerked out of her reverie. "Huh? Oh, you mean about not broadcasting the story about Hawkeye? No, I'm fine." She sat straighter, determined to remain professional. "Do you want another remote weather report or should I stay here at the station all day?"

Walt drummed his fingers on the surface of the desk before running a hand through his thick hair, mussing it worse than usual. "Stay for the noon report, do the six o'clock in front of that tea shop and I'll have the intern fill in at eleven."

"Tea for You? Again?" Wendy wondered why Walt thought people were so interested in the opening of a little spot like that in Bear Meadows.

Walt leaned back and clasped his hands behind his head. "The owner wants his tea brewing demonstration filmed. The last time you got distracted with the Betty story. This time stay on track. You said you want interviewing experience, and you're close to home."

When she didn't answer right away, Walt shrugged and said, "Whatcha gonna do?"

Wendy looked down at the Kilimanjaro photo. Walt still wanted her to combine weather with a fluff interview, but this could be her chance. She knew Joe Kowalsky brewed more than tea.

As soon as she finished with the noon report, she headed for Bear Meadows. She parked across the street from the coffee shop. She sat in the car watching the storeowners decorate the tiny strip mall. Of course, it was the day after Thanksgiving. Black Friday. The start of the holiday season.

Cheri, the owner of the consignment shop, hung lights along the banisters that edged the boardwalk in front of the storefronts. Her trademark hoop earrings sported tiny dangling Santa figures. Her long, dark curly hair was tied back with a red ribbon. She said something to Megan Martin, who stood, forefinger on chin, staring at a sleigh filled with colorfully wrapped boxes.

Wendy exited the car, crossed the street and walked up the steps. "Looks nice, ladies."

Megan slid the sleigh to the other side of her front door. "Thanks."

"Megan can't make up her mind. We'll be here all day if she doesn't get a move on." Cheri plugged in the lights and stood back as they lit. "Ta-da!"

"There's a right way and a wrong way. I want to balance the decorations so the eye is drawn."

"She has a point, Cheri." Standing nearby, Carolyn Hoffman painted a winter scene on the window of The Wildflower.

"You're so talented." Wendy remembered she was an art teacher. "Looks great."

"Thanks."

She left the three women discussing the merits of balance and entered the coffee shop. The overhead bell dinged when she opened the door. She was surprised to see Holly behind the counter. A sharp cry drew her attention to the seating area, where Louise sat, the two babies in carry seats on the table. Wendy felt no sweeping maternal urge to have a baby of her own, but she was happy to meet this little one. She looked down at the tiny infant. "So small."

"Not for long." Louise held her own two-month-old son in the crook of one arm while she held the other baby's bottle. "R.J. has already grown out of a lot of his clothes."

Wendy smiled. "What does R.J. stand for?"

"Robert for his dad and John for Mac because he's been so good to us."

Wendy walked to the counter. "And what did you name your little fella, Holly?"

"John, for his father. But we're calling him Jack." Holly was beaming watching the babies. "The usual?"

"If you're up to it. How are you feeling?"

"I'm doing okay. I'm only here for a couple of hours. Already I was missing adult company."

Wendy nodded. "Hi, Mrs. Hershberger." The former teacher waved to her.

"Hello, Wendy. What's the forecast for tomorrow?"

"Partly cloudy. Or maybe partly sunny. I get those two mixed up." As she had hoped, the comment coaxed a smile from the older woman. "How's your husband? Is he home yet?"

Mrs. Hershberger said, "He comes home tomorrow." She flipped through a magazine.

Watching her, Wendy got an idea. Walt's warning aside, she asked, "Mrs. Hershberger, could I interview you sometime?" The interview wouldn't garner national attention, but she had a feeling. The locals had loved the Riley interview, and everybody in town loved the retired teacher.

"Why would you want to do that? I'm not very interesting."

"You've taught hundreds of children." If nothing else, an interview might cheer the woman up.

"We'll see. I'll ask Hank what he thinks. If we do, he'll want to be out of the way."

"Is your husband afraid of being on camera? A lot of people get nervous when they're being filmed."

"It's not that. He was always so active before, when he ran the marina."

"He ran the marina out by the lake?"

"He used to." She closed her magazine. "Well, I should be getting home."

THE DAY AFTER THANKSGIVING, Josh was working alone on the cabin. He had left Wendy sometime after midnight. After two late nights in a row, he'd slept late this morning. So once he'd had a quick bite of breakfast, he'd taken stock of where he was. The stairs were almost complete. The banister still needed to be installed above, along the front of the loft. The cabin was suitable for just what it was intended for. A weekend retreat. No electricity. A green toilet. No running water, except the well outside. But that was okay, because he would soon be gone. And it would give his mom a place to hang out in the summer, when it would be more comfortable for her. It made him think of the rosebush by the front steps.

One more step to nail down and the stairs would be finished. Holding the nail in place with his left hand, he pounded the head once, feeling the vibration all the way up to his shoulder. He had to remind himself why he had left Montana.

He'd thought his mother was sick.

His mother wasn't sick. Not physically, anyway. She was humiliated. And his idea to try to get his parents back together had been a colossal failure. If he hadn't messed up so miserably in college, they wouldn't have had anything to argue about, and by extension, years later, maybe his father wouldn't have cheated on his mother, and they would still be living together. He pounded the nail again, this time hitting the head so hard the hammer left a mark in the wood. Well, he never claimed to be a carpenter, did he?

So why was he sticking around? For a girl who couldn't wait to get out of Bear Meadows? A girl who, if she really wanted to, could probably figure out his secret if she did any real digging. He stood, turned and threw the hammer, just missing the open door and his visitor.

"Whoa." Hawkeye threw up both arms to protect his face. "Guess I should've knocked. But then, I wasn't expecting flying hammers."

Josh's face reddened. "I'm sorry. I didn't hear anyone coming."

"You and the weather girl have a spat?"

"What makes you ask that?" He was annoyed at the question.

"My many years of bad judgment and missed chances."

Josh nodded.

The old farmer remained standing in the doorway, one hand still on the knob. "Joe and I brought you some railing."

"You did?" He felt even worse. "You shouldn't have."

"Your mother makes us some special bakery orders, so it wasn't any trouble. Besides, I'm hoping for an invitation to fish off the bank when the weather improves." He looked over his shoulder and then back at Josh, as if uncertain whether to stay or go. "Should we put it on the porch or...?"

Josh peered through the open door. Joe Kowalsky. Should he just leave things be? Leave his parents be? Forget about this town? "We may as well bring everything inside," he said and followed Hawkeye to the truck. "Thanks, Joe."

The next day, Hawkeye and Joe returned, and the three men worked together all day. Early afternoon, Skinny showed up with turkey sandwiches and iced tea. Skinny gave them a hand and three hours later, the cabin was as complete as they could make it. The stair treads and risers were installed. The recycled banister ran across the front of the loft and down the staircase. Except for furniture, there was nothing else for Josh to do. Thanking the men for their help, he watched them leave. Joe wasn't such a bad guy after all. His mother was an adult. It was time to let the chips fall where they may.

SUNDAY MORNING JOSH drove into town, knowing his mother would be at the bakery preparing the standard order for rolls for the nursing home. As soon as he opened the door, he was assailed by the aroma of fresh-baked bread.

"I'm closed," his mother called from the kitchen.

Josh went to find her. "You're such a warm, fuzzy kind of person, Mom, it's a wonder you don't have customers hanging out with you all day." He spied a cabbage on the counter.

Sue chuckled as she mixed rice into raw hamburger in a big bowl. "They don't have to like me, just my baking."

"Which they do." Josh peeked over her shoulder. "Halupkis?"

She nodded. "Skinny gave me a cabbage from his garden. He said they were partial to stuffed cabbage. Hint hint."

He kissed his mother on the cheek. "Do I get any?"

His mother laughed. "Of course."

Josh poured a cup of coffee, grabbed cookies from the counter and sat. "Joe and his uncles helped me finish the cabin yesterday."

"Really?" She turned to look at him as if for verification. At his nod, she turned and resumed her work. She peeled off a limp piece of cabbage and quickly rolled the meat in it, then put it in a roasting pan. "Finish? As in I can go up the stairs to the loft?"

"And hold on to a banister at the same time."

"Fantastic. So sweet of those boys to help. I'm glad I decided to make these today." His mom lifted the neatly rolled bundles of meat and cabbage into a casserole dish and poured a tomato mixture over the top. "These are going to take a while. Want to run up to the nursing home with me?"

"We'll take my truck."

By the time they had delivered the rolls and visited with a number of the residents, the stuffed cabbage was finished.

She wrapped the dish in a quilted carrier with a handle on top.

"I'll come with you." His mom seemed surprised, but said nothing.

They crossed the street and entered Tea for You. Josh was taken aback to see Wendy near the wall of glass jars with tea. Her camera was on the same tripod from a few days ago. The only other occupants were Deb and Bill, sipping tea at a corner table.

"Oh, I'm sorry, Joe. Are you busy?"

"Suzanna, come in, come in." He gave her a wide smile. "Especially if you're bringing what I think you're bringing."

"Hi, Josh." The female voice was one he'd remember for the rest of his life. Joe took the carrier dish from him and led Sue into the kitchen.

Josh turned and encountered a puzzled look from Wendy. He asked the first thing that popped into his head. "What are you doing here?"

"WHAT AM I DOING HERE? What are you doing here?" Wendy's hands shook. She hadn't expected such an audience for her blindside of Joe Kowalsky. But the mayor and her boyfriend had just happened to be passing by and thought they might like to try a new tea. And then here was Sue with something that smelled delicious in a casserole dish. And, of course Josh. Would he be happy or appalled with what she was about to do?

"I was just visiting my mom. Are you taping another interview?"

She nodded.

"Well, I'll get out of the way then. See you later."

"Josh, wait. You might want to watch this." She would take the risk that Josh would be satisfied to see the tea shop owner discredited in the eyes of his mother. *Which was worse? Infidelity or criminal behavior?*

"Why don't you stand behind the table with me, Wendy?" Joe smiled.

Wendy did so and held the microphone. "What do we need to know about teas?"

"Teas are at their best with the right temperature water, and different teas take different temperatures." He spooned a scoop of crumbled tea leaves into a diffuser. He drained hot water from a kettle sitting to one side.

"Chamomile tea is an example of an herbal tea. It's made from the flower and, if you drink it just before bed, can help you sleep. Herbal teas take a higher temperature than black or green teas and steep a bit longer." He handed the delicate china cup with the fragrant tea to Wendy with a smile. "Would you like to try?"

"Delicious." She watched as Joe prepared other varieties of teas and discussed each one.

"You seem comfortable in front of the camera, Joe. Have you done this before?"

He laughed and shook his head. "Tea for You is my first commercial business."

"You worked for a large bank in Pittsburgh. Didn't you do a lot of presentations in your position as a mortgage loan officer?"

Joe held a cup under the spout of the teapot. He made no facial reaction. The tea he was pouring overfilled the cup and spilled onto the saucer. Suddenly, Joe's hand jerked, and hot water hit the table-cloth. He looked up at the camera, as if to see whether the light was still on. Then he studied Wendy. His friendly expression was gone. He looked as if he had fallen for a trap, which he had. "I don't think my former occupation is relevant to the tea business."

Wendy pushed on. Her instincts hummed. *Secrets out in threes.* And here she was with number two. If she didn't get the words out, he would disappear into the back room and her chance would be lost.

"Joe, Mr. Kowalsky…" She pulled the Pittsburgh paper out of the briefcase at her feet. "This paper from last year says you were implicated in a fraud scheme at the bank." She spread the paper on the cloth-covered table.

Joe appeared sick. Wendy had often seen the expression on the faces of the people her sister had interviewed. He had been caught. This was it. She had her story. Joe just stared down at the headline.

"You were named as an accomplice by

Vanessa Black, another employee of the bank where you worked."

She tilted the microphone toward Joe's lips. But he had gone to that place in his mind he went the last time she interviewed him. His face was blank.

"Is it true you and the accused, Vanessa Black, are engaged to be married?"

CHAPTER ELEVEN

"FRAUD? ENGAGED? JOE, what is she talking about?" Sue looked up at the man, whose face was as white as the color of the table-cloth. "And who's Vanessa? Is this some sort of joke?"

The look in Joe's eyes told everyone Wendy's accusations were no joke. "Suzanna, I can explain."

Sue's voice was soft. "You wouldn't steal from innocent people."

The room was so quiet you could've heard a tea bag drop. Joe, having no good answer, disappeared into the back room. The only sound was the scraping of chairs as Deb and Bill stood. They walked over and glanced down at the paper.

Bill looked at Deb and said, "Number two." Deb just shook her head, took Bill by the arm and together they exited the shop.

That left Josh, his mother and Wendy, who was busy putting away her equipment.

His mother rested a hand on his arm as if for support. "I guess there really is no such thing as a good man." She smiled sadly and then patted his cheek. "Except you." She turned and headed for the door.

Josh's heart flopped in his chest. If she only knew. He wasn't sure how to react to the last few minutes. One thing he knew though, Wendy wasn't some innocent local journalist reporting on lost puppies and county fairs. Skinny had been right. She was looking for the big ticket to propel her to stardom. Unluckily for Joe, he could very well turn out to be said ticket.

Josh walked over and looked down at the wrinkled Pittsburgh newspaper. A bold headline ran across the top of the page:

LOCAL BANKER IMPLICATED IN SCAM

Underneath the text was a picture of Joe smiling up from the page.

Josh skimmed the entire article. Due to a lack of evidence, Joe had been released, while Vanessa Black had been convicted and sentenced. Josh threw the paper on the table. "So this is what you do."

Wendy knelt and stuck the camera into a black bag. Then she folded the tripod and put it into a side pocket. "Aren't you happy? Your mother could never care for a man who's committed a criminal act. Now that she's no longer interested in Joe, maybe she'll find a way to forgive your father and they'll get back together."

"You're a weather girl."

"For the last time, I am not a weather girl. I am a weather—" She seemed to be searching for the right word. "Weather forecaster."

"All the same, I didn't know you did these ambush-style interviews."

Wendy looked startled. Well, maybe Josh didn't wear suits and work in an office, but he had been around.

"How did you find out about this?"

"I'm a reporter. That's what I do."

"Let me ask the question another way. Who gave you the newspaper?"

Wendy had been busily stuffing cords and other items in the black canvas bag, but at his question, her hands stilled.

Josh flashed on the memory of Wendy in his grandmother's rocker after Thanksgiving dinner, talking to his father. For a man whose wife had left him and reconciliation was nowhere on the horizon, he looked happy relaxing in the recliner. When Josh walked into the room, she had been stuffing something into her purse. The newspaper. "My father."

"Yes. But I thought this might mean she'd give your father a second chance. That's what you wanted, right?"

Now he knew how his father had met the new librarian. He had been doing research. Josh caught a glimpse of his mom through the window. She was slowly climbing the steps to the bakery, her shoulders bowed as if she carried a heavy load. "Not like this." Thinking she might need to talk, he turned and started for the door.

"What about the matches?"

Josh stopped next to the register, where the Tiffany lamp gave a cheerful glow to the polished wood counter. "What matches?" He glanced at the window again, not wanting to look at Wendy anymore. But he couldn't help himself. He met her unflinching gaze. "What matches?" he repeated.

"The matches at the cabin. On the mantel. The ones you start fires with. Haven't you ever looked at them?"

He huffed out a breath. "I don't know what you're talking about."

"Sue and Brad. Gold script on a pink background. Matches from your parents' wedding."

The matches he'd found in a drawer and used to start fires at the cabin. Not once did he look at the cover. Josh ran his fingers across the top of the counter and thought of Joe helping him install the railing across the front of the loft. Joe Kowalsky did nice work. Maybe he should get out of the tea business and try woodworking. "Your parents were happy once."

Josh shook his head and found himself returning Wendy's hard gaze. "You know what, Miss Valentine? Maybe you should just mind your own business." He left, slamming the door behind him.

"No? Are you kidding me?" This time instead of getting the news over the phone,

Wendy sat directly across from the station manager in his cluttered office. She had waited until finishing the morning broadcast before she'd approached Walt. They had watched the interview together.

"Apparently he's in the clear." Walt rocked back and forth, gazing up at the drop ceiling.

Wendy was so frustrated she thought about screaming. She was sure Walt would be receptive to the story. Joe Kowalsky was involved in bank fraud, and he ran away to hide in Bear Meadows. "But he was charged."

"And then released." Walt continued to rock. "Either they don't have enough evidence, or he's innocent. Either way, there's no story."

Taking a deep breath, Wendy released the stranglehold her fingers had on her chair. She wouldn't have been surprised if her fingertips had left dents in the wood. "Fine." She stood and headed for the door, steaming.

"Do you know why I'm here, Wendy?"

She stopped abruptly. The boss wasn't finished with her.

Turning, she eyed the older man. "No."

"Sixty-five years old and I'm at a tiny station in central Pennsylvania."

Walt's rocking was starting to get on her nerves, and she suspected she was in for a lesson. She crossed her arms, leaned back against the frosted glass of the door. "I don't know, Walt. You must want to be here."

"Are you kidding? I want to be in Seattle. These mountains make me claustrophobic. I grew up on the West Coast. I should finish out my career there."

She had been so sure. First that Josh would appreciate the truth about Joe and second that Walt would want to air it. The guy was a charlatan. Walt seemed to be waiting for a response. "So why aren't you in Seattle? There must be stations there like WSHF. You're talented, loads of experience."

Walt sat forward and rested his heavy arms on the paper-strewed desk. "I aired a story about an important businessman accused of assault. Turns out it was a case of mistaken identity. Took a while to clear up. Lucky for the guy he had an ironclad alibi. And because I ran with the story so I could beat the competition, I didn't verify my sources. The station was sued. I was out of a job. Being unemployed eats through the savings quicker than you might think." He picked up the shot glass. "And this little souvenir reminds me every day I might have started drinking a little bit too much. So here I am, in Shadow Falls, Pennsylvania, waiting to retire."

"I'm sorry." Wendy stared at the cluttered cardboard box next to the chair.

"Live and learn."

The photo of Walt with Mount Kilimanjaro in the background stared back at her. "So you're not airing the interview at the tea shop."

Walt shook his head. "Not even the part about how to brew the perfect cup of tea."

JOSH HAD RETURNED to the cabin after Wendy's exposé. His mother for once didn't seem to want him around and begged off, saying she had a headache. Since the cabin was finished, he spent all day Monday sweeping up sawdust and polishing the surfaces. Nobody came by. Not that he expected anyone. Joe wouldn't want to be seen. Hawkeye would be closing ranks around a family member. And Wendy would be busy looking for her next victim.

Despite what she'd done to Hawkeye and Joe, he admired the young woman. Another time, another place, and they might have become an item. Running a cloth along the top of the mantel, he stopped when he came to the pack of matches Wendy had mentioned. Gold script on a pink background. Sue and Brad. A souvenir of a happier time indeed.

His parents would have to work things out for themselves, if ever. He was just relieved that his mom wasn't sick. So the time had come to head back out west. He would continue at his friend's ranch until another opportunity presented itself.

Tuesday morning he tidied the cabin and packed up the truck. He felt some satisfaction that the cabin was a little more habitable than when he had first arrived. One final check on his mother. He went by the house, knowing his father would be at a job site, showered, found some clean clothes and then drove to The Cookie Jar. His mom would be baking whether she wanted to or not. She had orders to fill, and she wouldn't let down her customers for love nor money. Or lack of love.

Parking in front of the bakery, he climbed the stairs and then stopped. He turned. Tea for You was dark. He felt bad for the tea shop owner. *We all make mistakes. Sometimes we get caught, sometimes we don't.* A little voice in the back of his head said *we always get caught.* Josh wondered.

He entered the shop and heard the rattling of pans in the kitchen. Rounding the counter, he followed the noise. "Hi, Mom."

Her back to him, his mom jumped at his words. "I didn't hear you come in." After a quick smile, she returned to the bread dough on a floured board. Her shoulders worked as she kneaded and flipped the mound of dough. "If you want coffee, help yourself. The nursing home asked for an extra order of rolls. They're having a special dinner this evening."

"Thanks." Josh grabbed a flowered mug from the shelf, the twin to the one at his cabin, and poured himself a cup of coffee. He eyed a box of pastries. His stomach growled, and he remembered he hadn't eaten yet. "Can I have a glazed doughnut?"

His mother nodded. She flipped the dough into a bowl and covered it with a towel. Then she poured herself a cup of coffee and sat down opposite him. "Good?"

He nodded, his mind on how to tell his mother he was leaving. "I should—"

"I'm so glad we've had this much time together...despite everything. I've missed you, Josh. I'm glad you're okay." She patted his hand. "Are you okay?"

Josh pulled his hand away and got up under the pretense of taking his dishes to the sink. "Sure. I have plenty of money. I like being outdoors, the ranch is pretty cool. Did you see my new truck?"

"Of course. You took Joe and me to the church, remember?"

Josh nodded, thinking of the night of the blizzard. That seemed like ages ago. "It's a great vehicle, has all the bells and whistles."

"Well, how about you and that fancy vehicle do some deliveries for me?"

Josh looked for a clock, knowing it was

getting late. "I was planning on getting an early start." Her face fell at his response. He took a deep breath. "Okay, what do you need, Mom?"

"I have a box of chicken salad sandwiches—"

"Yum. Your homemade bread?" Josh peered into the box at the perfect triangles.

"Absolutely."

"Any leftovers?"

"Unfortunately, no." His mom retrieved two more boxes from the far counter and set them on the table. "A box of raisin-filled cookies and one of assorted."

Josh rubbed his stomach, which, despite the doughnut, had begun to growl. "Where to? The nursing home?" He could still be on the road by noon.

"Mrs. Hershberger's. The ladies from the church are meeting."

Josh's heart sank. "Mrs. Hershberger? Now? Maybe I should do the delivery to the nursing home and you can take Mrs. Hershberger's order. She lives closer."

His mother looked at him oddly, her brow wrinkled. "You have a problem going to the Hershberger home?"

"No, it's just..." What could he say? He had no choice but to carry the boxes out and put them on the front seat of his truck and drive the few blocks to the home of the retired teacher. He could be in and out quickly.

The tiny ranch house was outside the main business square of Bear Meadows. A white-picket fence surrounded a small lawn that still had traces of the big snow. A Go Bears sign stood perched in the flowerbed.

He unlatched the gate and walked up the sidewalk. He transferred the boxes to one arm so he could use the other hand to knock on the door. He waited. No sound came from inside. He looked around and debated leaving the boxes on the porch. He knocked again.

When the door opened, he expected to see the retired first-grade teacher, dressed in her signature pink tracksuit. Instead, he found himself looking down.

"And who might you be?" His expression disgruntled, a broad-shouldered man with thinning hair sat in a wheelchair. Hank Hershberger.

The man he had almost killed was alive.

But certainly not well.

CHAPTER TWELVE

FOR A MOMENT Josh feared his lungs had collapsed because all the air seemed to have left his body. The boxes would've landed on the Happy Holidays welcome mat at his feet if he hadn't taken a step back.

The man gripped the armrests and leaned forward in his wheelchair. His eyes narrowed. "Are you deaf? What do you want?"

Before Josh could answer, Mrs. Hershberger appeared. One hand covered two pink rollers at her forehead. "This is Sue and Brad Hunter's boy. You brought my goodies, didn't you, Josh? You're such a sweetheart. Move back so the boy can get in the door, Hank."

Hank wheeled backward. But his expression was decidedly less welcome than his wife's.

"The ladies will be here any minute, and I'm not ready yet." Waving a hand, she pointed down the hallway. "Just put the boxes on the kitchen table." She disappeared through a door.

With a nod to the husband, he hurried into the kitchen and set the boxes on a metal table, which could have been the twin to the one in his mother's bakery. He couldn't get out of the house soon enough. But when he turned to leave, the doorway was blocked.

The man in the wheelchair looked him up and down. Josh must have passed inspection. "Cup of coffee?" Mr. Hershberger wheeled past Josh and stretched to reach the pot on the back of the stove. "I keep telling Vera not to push the pot to the back burner, but she never listens." He sat back, disgusted. "I think she's afraid I'll spill it on myself." He motioned to his skinny legs and laughed. "Not like I'll feel anything."

The kitchen was small, but, even so, Josh felt as if the walls were closing in. He wanted nothing more than to run away from the man staring at the pot on the back of the stove. "I'll get it."

"There's two travel cups in that corner cupboard. Let's get out of here before those church ladies show up." Hank wheeled over to the table and inspected the boxes.

Josh poured the coffee and snapped the lids on the cups. "My mom said your wife asked for two dozen sandwiches."

"She always gets more than she needs. She won't miss them." He loaded up a plate with four sandwiches and a half-dozen cookies and balanced the plate on his lap. With a conspiratorial grin, he tipped his head toward the back door. "Follow me."

Josh glanced down the hall. His escape was only feet away. Instead, he picked up the cups and followed the man. Mr. Hershberger wheeled himself down a ramp and onto a wide concrete pathway.

Josh followed him to a large garage at the farthest part of the yard. Hank disappeared through the wide double doors. Josh took one last look at the pathway and the gate leading to the front of the house. His plan to leave town had crumbled. Well, what was one more hour or two?

Josh entered the dark garage and spied Hank at a cluttered workbench. The air smelled of turpentine and grease. He set Hank's cup close enough that the man could reach it.

"I'll take one of the sandwiches, and you help yourself. Looks like you've missed a few meals." Mr. Hershberger passed him the plate and again looked Josh over head to toe. "You a military man?"

"I was."

"I thought so. The way you carry yourself. I had it, too, in my day." He shook his head. "Come look at this." He led Josh to the back of the garage. "Flip on that light switch."

The last thing Josh expected to see at Christmastime in Bear Meadows was a boat under construction. This was no small project. The vessel had to be about twenty feel long. "You built this?" He walked around the vessel. Up on cribbing, the hull was at eye level. He ran a hand along the edge, sanded down to bare wood.

"She's an antique, son. A 1949 classic luxury item. I bought her from a guy in Florida ten years ago."

Josh continued to examine the boat. She certainly was beautiful. The seats were red upholstery. The dash was a rich mahogany. Then Hank's words sunk in. "You bought the boat to restore."

"Yep."

Josh felt sick. He looked at the half-finished sandwich in his hand. He was at the stern of the boat now, out of Hank's sight. He leaned over, breathing deep. He should have left town.

"She'll hold up to eight people. I thought I'd take her over to the lake. I used to have a marina there. Look at that hull. Man, I'll bet she'll skim across the water." His last sentence had been full of wistfulness. "Hey, where'd you get to, fella?"

"Just admiring your craftsmanship." Josh walked back to the bow.

"She's a beauty, isn't she?" For the first time since their encounter at the front door, Hank Hershberger smiled. He wheeled slowly around the boat, running his hand along the side. "A 1949 seventeen-foot run-about. The trailer's over there in the other corner."

"But how…"

"I bought her before my accident. I've got everything done except painting the outer hull. White with red trim. What do you think?"

Josh looked away. "Sounds good."

"I guess it doesn't matter anymore. The next owner can paint her any color he or she wants. I don't suppose you're in the market?"

Josh shook his head, unable to speak. Not enough that he had put a person in a wheelchair, he had destroyed his dream. He recalled seeing Mrs. Hershberger's little car. Without thinking, he asked, "What were you going to pull the boat with?"

"I used to have a three-quarter-ton pickup. Couldn't drive anymore. So what was the point?" He sighed. Josh spied a set of weights in the corner, covered with dust. "Whose weights?"

"Mine." Hank laughed. "After the accident, they said I should work out to maintain my upper body strength. I did for a while. But again…what's the point?

"I'm glad you brought Vera's delivery, son. I don't get to talk to many young people anymore. And Fritz Hoffman used to come around, but after he and Rose bought that Victorian he's kept busy with repairs."

Josh rested a hand on the hull of the boat.

A trusting man, Dr. Reed always left the keys in the car's ignition. Josh opened the garage door, glancing around in the gathering dusk for potential witnesses to his deed. The mansion and the garage with the second-floor apartment were set far back from the main street and hidden in a century's old grove of oak trees. He settled on the leather seat and inserted the key. Thanks to the hours the two men had spent, the engine turned over instantly. Josh couldn't tell if the warm glow deep inside came from driving the car or was left over from the whiskey he had consumed in the den. It didn't matter. The memories of his disagreement with his father faded, and he pulled into the alley behind the house and drove out of town. Knowing the red car was easily recognized, he headed toward the cabin. When he got to Little Bear Creek, he didn't want to stop. The night was beautiful. A crescent moon lay just above the horizon, the evening star crisp against the azure western sky. He made it to Last Chance Road, less likely to be seen, and sped down the narrow road. He was watching the rest of the stars come into sight in the night sky, still lit from the setting sun. On the road, night had already fallen thanks to the pine trees lining both sides. He had been looking up at the moon when he felt the sudden thump. His heart leaped into his chest. He slowed just in time to see a deer leap across the road. What were the odds? The one time he took Dr. Reed's car for a spin without permission... and he had hit a deer.

"It's safe to come in now, boys." Josh turned at the sound of Mrs. Hershberger's voice. He glanced at the clock over the workbench. A big fish seemed to jump out between the nine and the three, caught by a fisherman in the background. That's how he felt. He was hooked. He had been talking to Hank for two hours.

"The church ladies gone, Vera?"

"Yes, dear. And don't think I didn't know you lifted a couple sandwiches." She approached the boat. "What have you two been up to this whole time?"

"Talking about boats, the service. Josh just got out of the military. What branch were you in, son?"

Josh wished the man would stop calling him son. "Army."

Hank chuckled. "No wonder you didn't know what kind of boat this is."

The retired teacher gave him an appraising look. "I knew you'd joined the military, but I couldn't remember what branch. That's nice that you two have something in common then." She nodded, a thoughtful expression on her face. "Supper's almost ready, Hank. Why don't you go on in and wash up. Would you like to stay, Josh?"

Watching Hank wheel across the concrete floor reminded Josh of what he had done. "Thanks, Mrs. Hershberger, but I have plans." He started to follow Hank out the door, but Mrs. Hershberger grabbed his elbow with a viselike grip. "Josh."

He grimaced. *Did she know? Could she see it on his face?* The woman had always had an uncanny ability of knowing what her students were up to, sometimes before they did.

"I've got to go."

"Wait, Josh. I want to thank you."

"For what?"

"For spending time out here in this dirty

old shop with Hank. He hasn't been away from the television this long in years. If I'd known that's all it took, I would've hired someone to come talk boats with him ages ago." She still held on to his sleeve, and a note of desperation crept into her voice. "Maybe you could come back while you're home? I could pay you to help Hank work on the boat."

"I'll see, Mrs. Hershberger." Josh gave her a grim smile and patted the hand still clutching his sleeve. But right now...he couldn't get away fast enough.

WENDY WENT THROUGH the rest of the week like a robot. She didn't hear from Josh at all. After their last encounter, maybe it was just as well. Maybe it was for the better. She did the weather in the studio and on Friday did a remote from the bridge over Little Bear Creek. When she finished, she stood on the bridge and looked in the direction of the cabin. All she could see was part of the roofline and the chimney. No smoke was coming out.

At home, she sat on the back porch and considered her options.

Should she take the job at the local Miami station? She could go to sea as a broadcast technician. Somehow the thought of being at sea wasn't appealing. Or there was that move to Burbank and being a spot producer.

The argument with Josh had bothered her more than she realized. Instead of appreciating what she had done, Josh had disapproved. He was an up-front kind of guy. He pulled no punches. He wouldn't have sabotaged Joe the way she had done. But then, he wasn't a reporter, either.

Maybe she should forget about following in her sister's footsteps. Maybe she should just be happy where she was. Maybe she could have a boyfriend. She already had the dog.

She would do things Walt's way for a while. She would interview Mrs. Hershberger for a nice piece about the beloved, retired teacher. Like her interview with Riley McAndrews, the piece would make people feel good. And maybe she could ask her about the weather in Antarctica. Walt would appreciate that.

CHAPTER THIRTEEN

THE CAMERA WAS already set up, focused on the armchair perpendicular to the couch. She hadn't widened the view so they both could be seen. Now, wandering around the old-fashioned living room while waiting for her hostess, Wendy peered at a photo on the polished surface of the upright piano in the corner of the living room.

Mrs. Hershberger was in the kitchen, having insisted on serving tea and cookies while Wendy interviewed her. In the photo, the slim young woman with dark curls wore a long white dress. The train draped around her feet like the petals of a flower. Mrs. Hershberger had been a beautiful bride. Next to her stood a broad-shouldered man in uniform.

Walt had agreed to the interview, although given Wendy's previous experience, he was making no promises. But then, he had nothing to lose. She was conducting the interview on her own time. Sunday afternoon. Outside a freezing rain fell, but inside the house was warm and cozy. She ran her fingers over the ivory keys and found middle C.

"Do you play?" Mrs. Hershberger set a silver tray on the coffee table in front of the couch.

Wendy laughed. "I only lasted a year. Then I started playing soccer, and that was the end of piano lessons." She perched on the edge of the overstuffed floral couch. She feared if she sat farther back she would sink so far into the cushions she wouldn't be able to get up.

"There's milk and sugar, if you like. I'm afraid I don't have any lemon." Mrs. Hershberger handed her a floral cup and saucer. "In my day, most girls took piano lessons. We didn't have the availability of sports like they do now."

Wendy added a splash of milk to her cup. "Really? I guess I never thought about it. Times have changed."

"They have." The retired teacher sat in the matching chair. "As much as I like having company, I'm not sure I have anything of value to share."

"Let me be the judge of that, Mrs. Hershberger."

"Call me Vera."

Balancing her cup in one hand, Wendy reached up and turned on the camera. "Why don't we start with why you became a teacher?"

Vera glanced up at the camera, then down at the cup in her hand. Wendy was accustomed to people being shy around cameras. Her job was to make them forget the camera was there. "Have you always liked children?"

"Actually, no."

Here we go.

"Being the youngest in a family of six, I wasn't accustomed to being around little ones. I planned to teach science at the high school level. I was in my third year at Florida State when I got a job working with a young boy who had been blind from birth."

Wendy leaned forward. "Wait a minute. You're from Florida? I thought you went to Penn State."

"I earned my master's at Penn State, and

I'm originally from Delaware. That's where I met Hank. We were childhood sweethearts, you might say."

Forgetting how soft the cushions were, Wendy leaned back, sinking deep into the sofa. She glanced at the camera, wondering if her imitation of a turtle on its back was being filmed. Major editing would need to be done. Balancing her cup on the couch's arm, she scooted forward. When she was once more upright, she retrieved her cup. *Where was she?* Oh right, discovering that there was more to the retired teacher than she had realized.

"You went to Florida even though Hank lived in Delaware?"

"Hank was in the Coast Guard and gone most of the time. We managed to see each other enough to keep the sparks flying." She smiled. "I spent a summer helping Roger prepare for public school. After that summer, I changed my major to elementary education. I never looked back."

Wendy was amazed. "Do you know what happened to Roger?"

The teacher nodded, a proud smile on her face. "He started his own software company. He's asked Hank and I to come to Florida for years. First we were both busy working, and then after the accident…" Her enthusiasm seemed to deflate like air out of a child's balloon.

Wendy's mind buzzed. So many threads to follow. And she thought this interview would be boring. Then she remembered a conversation between Holly and Louise. "Did you go to Antarctica last year?"

The woman blushed. "Silly, isn't it? Old lady like me."

"Are you kidding? I think it's fabulous." Without even realizing she was doing it, she glanced around the living room at the out-of-date furniture.

"The senior class paid for the trip."

Wendy felt heat from embarrassment creep into her cheeks. "I didn't mean to…"

"We don't have the money for trips like that. Last year's senior class remembered me talking about wanting to do a trip when they were in first grade. Can you believe it? They did a fund-raiser for me. I was just flabbergasted. I wasn't going to go, but Hank insisted. He said I might never have another opportunity."

"You're still interested in science, aren't you?"

Vera nodded. "Now that I have time, I research environmental issues that have always fascinated me. The ocean, for one. Hank used to tell me such stories of the things he observed out at sea. I saw a story on the news the other night about a fish that can be trained to recognize a human face. That's fascinating, don't you think?"

Wendy nodded. She had seen the same show. Her sister had done an interview with a member of the British royal family earlier in the program.

"Wait a minute. She's your sister, isn't she?" Vera looked as if she had just put two and two together. "Rose mentioned something about your sister being a well-known reporter, but I didn't figure it out until now. Your sister is Katie Valentine."

Wendy set her empty cup on the table and picked up her tablet. She had just lost momentum. The death knell to any good interview. Maybe she should stick to the weather. "Yes, Mrs. Hershberger—"

"Vera."

"Vera. Katie is my sister."

"I can see the resemblance. You're both such lovely looking women. I just remembered. I have a photo album from my trip. Come with me."

Putting the camera on pause, Wendy hefted it and the tripod, and accompanied her hostess to the kitchen.

"Have a seat." She pulled a photo album from a bookshelf and laid it on the table. "This is the ship I was on. They converted a research vessel into a passenger cruise ship."

Wendy pushed the On button. "When did you go?"

"January is their summer. We saw whales, fur seals, baby chicks. The Antarctica peninsula has long days. We could read a newspaper on deck at midnight." She glanced out the kitchen window. "Oh my goodness."

Wendy looked up at the sound of alarm in Vera's voice and followed the woman's gaze to the window. An elderly man in a wheelchair, clearly freezing from the icy rain, inched his way from a garage to a ramp leading into the house. She recognized the square jaw. The man in the wheelchair was the broad-shouldered groom in the wedding photograph. But now he was drenched.

"Please, Joshua. It would mean so much to me."

How could he refuse Mrs. Hershberger? The answer was he couldn't. So for the remainder of the week he had been spending time with the teacher's wheelchair-bound husband, putting two coats of paint on the boat. In between coats of paint, he had dusted off the weights and generally straightened up the man's workshop. Almost five days had passed since he'd loaded up the pickup to leave. Maybe Hank would never put his boat in the water and skim across the lake, but at least when he sold it he would get the most money for it.

"I thought you'd be gone by now." Brad Hunter stood in the doorway of Josh's old bedroom.

"It's not for lack of trying." Josh stared at the collection of things in his closet. A baseball bat. Textbooks. Odd and ends of his teenage years. After the shock of seeing Hank Hershberger confined to a wheelchair, Josh had needed an escape. He had tried fishing, but couldn't seem to relax. Today with the freezing rain, fishing was out. He had finally succumbed to cabin fever. With nowhere else to go, he had gone home.

"Or did you come back for your stuff? Like your mother wants to."

Josh reached for his baseball mitt. He shoved his hand into it, feeling the soft leather against his fingers. Those innocent days were so long ago. He pounded his fist into the palm. "If you don't mind, I'd just as soon leave everything right where it is." He suddenly remembered his mother mentioning his father moving to Colorado with the girlfriend. Maybe he still planned to go, girlfriend or not. "You're not moving, are you?"

"I thought about moving, but things didn't work out." His father shook his head. "Want a burger?"

Josh nodded. His father walked away, and Josh closed the closet door and followed him to the kitchen. "Don't you get tired of hamburgers?"

"I'm not much of a cook."

Josh sat. "Listen, I wanted to tell you something the other day."

"That you can't stand to be around me? Yeah, I got the message." A cast-iron skillet dropped on the stove with a clang.

"No, Dad, that's not it at all."

The meat began to sizzle.

Josh pulled two more of the Valentines' cherry sodas from the refrigerator and put the bag of chips on the table without asking his father. Waiting for the hamburgers to be ready, Josh noticed all trace of his mother had disappeared from the familiar kitchen.

"So what did you want to tell me?"

Josh stared down at his plate. Eight years he had kept the secret. Eight years he hadn't told anyone what he'd done. "That night in May when I asked you for the car and you said no. Remember?"

Brad nodded. "You keep bringing that up. I didn't think it was that big of a deal. Lots of parents refuse—"

"I took Dr. Reed's car out." He glanced up to see his father's reaction.

His dad's face was impassive. "You two took the car out quite a bit, as I remember.

Dr. Reed liked you. That was part of the reason I let you handle the contract."

"Dr. Reed was at a conference in Philadelphia that night." Josh cleared his throat. "I took the car out alone."

Brad's eyes lit with awareness. "Uh-huh. You dent it up a little? I heard the doctor's daughter is selling the car. You feeling a little guilty because it's not mint anymore?"

Josh shook his head. "No. I mean, yes, I damaged the car some, but I fixed it."

"Fair enough. No one will ever be the wiser. No harm, no foul."

Josh pushed back his chair and walked over to the sink. He looked out the kitchen window. The bird feeder hanging in the maple tree in the backyard was empty. He wondered when it had been filled last. At the far end of the property was his father's garage where all his lawn care equipment was kept. The garage was about the same size as Hank Hershberger's. The two men were similar in a way. Physical men, with lots of hobbies and outdoor activities. "I hit somebody." Behind him he heard his father reach into the chip bag.

"What are you talking about? When?"

"That night. The night I asked you for the car." Josh turned and leaned back against the sink. He thrust his hands into his pockets and shut his eyes. "I hit Hank Hershberger."

"Hey, man, where you been all week-end? I thought we were going to play a little ball." Tony Gabriel slammed shut his locker door and turned to eye best friends Susie and Marcia as they walked past him in the hall. Tony couldn't seem to make up his mind who he liked better so he flirted with them both.

Josh usually told his best friend everything. This time he didn't. He had worked all day Sunday fixing the dent in the right front fender of the classic car. As long as nobody went into the garage until the paint dried, he was home free. "I had stuff to do at Dr. Reed's."

Tony knew Josh maintained the grounds at the mansion. "Your old man put you to work. That figures."

Josh thought it a good story, so went with it.

"Hey, you hear about the hit-and-run?"

"What are you talking about?" Josh asked.

"Somebody hit Mrs. Hershberger's husband Saturday night."

"No kidding? That's too bad. She's my favorite teacher."

"She's everybody's favorite teacher." They walked across the hall and entered homeroom. Tony's gaze immediately sought out Susie. He and Josh sat in the back of the room. Josh pulled out the book he was to be reading for English lit. Maybe he could get a chapter done. He was halfway through the chapter when he heard the words *Last Chance Road.* He looked up. The homeroom teacher stood at the door talking with the math teacher. He strained to listen.

"...always go on a walk right after supper, but she had papers to grade. She didn't even know he was hit until Chief Stone came to the door."

"I heard he's in a coma. Not expected to live." The math teacher looked over his shoulder toward his classroom across the hall. His eyes widened in alarm, and he

rushed away. Josh could hear him admonishing the students to get back to work.

Josh's heart seized. He had hit a deer. He was sure of it. He slipped a scrap of paper in his book and walked up to the teacher's desk. "Did Mrs. Hershberger's husband have a heart attack?"

The woman shook her head. "He was hit by a car. The scumbag didn't even stop to see if he was okay. Just left him there in the road. Who could do something like that?"

His father stood frozen at the stove. "You didn't know you hit him?" The burgers sizzled away, unnoticed.

Josh shook his head. "I thought I hit a deer. Did you know Hank?"

Running one hand over his face, his father nodded. "He had a nice business running the marina at the lake. I never saw a man more at home on the water. I think he was in the Coast Guard for a while." His father sighed, then looked down at the skillet. "Well, nothing you can do about it now."

Josh straightened. "You don't think I need to confess?"

"Are you kidding? You could go to jail." His father checked the burgers, pushing them around in the skillet. "You know, I wondered."

Josh peered at his father, who avoided his gaze. The hamburgers no longer smelled good. "You wondered what, Dad?" He should've talked to Matt back in Montana, or someone else here. Maybe Hawkeye would've given him a logical answer, one based on common sense.

His dad's jaw tightened. He carried the skillet of burned meat to the garbage can, tossed it in and then walked over to the window. "Those birds are probably missing your mother."

Josh kept his silence. Was his father really talking about the birds? Brad Hunter was a man who kept his thoughts and feelings inside. If Josh interrupted now, he might never know what his father had wondered about. And he had to know. So he waited.

Brad rattled the faucet. "I've been meaning to tighten this." Then, as if his mind were made up, he walked over to Josh and rested his hands on his shoulders. "That weekend Hank Hershberger ended up in the hospital…you changed. I thought maybe it was because all you kids had his wife for first grade and liked her so much. But after a week or so, the other kids went back to normal." He squeezed Josh's shoulders. "You didn't."

Josh raised his head and met his father's gaze. His voice was quiet. "Why didn't you ask?"

"I hoped I was wrong. I thought maybe the change in you was because your mother and I weren't getting along. I guess I should have asked. Maybe you wouldn't have gone through all the turmoil you've had."

Josh reached up and rested his hand on his father's. "If it's any consolation, I doubt it would have made any difference."

"Listen, why don't you stay here until you're ready to leave?" His dad squeezed his shoulders, which was as close to a hug as he could get. "You remember where we hide the key, don't you?"

"Third flowerpot to the left. I remember, Dad."

His father grinned sheepishly. "We should probably change that, huh?"

Josh shook his head. "I'll be back,

Dad. Right now I need to clear my head. Thanks."

Ten minutes later he was on his way back to the cabin. He kept seeing Hank Hersh-berger in the wheelchair. What if it had been his father? An outdoors man, accus-tomed to being active, coming and going easily under his own steam. By the time he reached the turnoff, Josh felt numb. The truck wasn't going much more than twenty miles an hour when Josh stomped on the brakes, spotting an animal in the middle of the road. Rover, the stray black Lab with the brown paws. He wore a knowing smile.

"No." Josh struck the steering wheel with the heel of his hand. "You're on your own, dog. I've been in this town too long al-ready. Now get out of the way." He tapped the horn to emphasize his point.

The dog continued to smile.

Leaning his forehead against the steer-ing wheel, Josh shut his eyes. Nothing was turning out how he had hoped. Not his par-ents' marriage, not slipping in and out of town, and not—

He lifted his head and stared at the dog. Had he really been hoping something would happen between him and the weather girl, or news reporter, or whatever she called herself? If he was, then he was definitely delusional because Wendy Valentine had mapped out her life a long time ago, and it didn't include him. He, Josh Hunter, was directionless, or, as Hank Hershberger might say, rudderless. He smiled grimly and then leaned over and opened the passenger door.

The dog trotted forward and jumped onto the seat as if this were something he did every day. He lay down and rested his chin on Josh's thigh. Chocolate brown eyes stared up at his rescuer in appreciation.

Josh ran his hand over the smooth dome. "The only reason I'm doing this is to say goodbye."

Josh backed up, crossed the bridge and turned right onto Last Chance Road. He would return the dog, say his goodbyes, make sure the cabin was secure and set out for Interstate 80 West.

But when the back door to the ranch house opened, only the first part of his plan took place. The dog slipped past him and disappeared down the hall. Before Josh could say a word, a meaty hand grabbed him by the wrist and pulled him into the kitchen.

CHAPTER FOURTEEN

WENDY SAT WITH closed eyes in front of the fireplace, her feet on a tufted hassock. The freezing rain had since moved east, but she hadn't finished the interview with Vera Hershberger. Hank had needed help with the wheelchair. His wife was frantic he would come down with pneumonia again. Vera had mentioned an accident. She must have been referring to the injury that had caused her husband to require the wheelchair.

Suddenly the sounds of dogs barking out "Jingle Bells" drifted down the hall.

Bernie and Babs were home finally and were having a good old time in the kitchen trying out recipes for their upcoming annual Christmas party. She took a deep breath and imagined she was in the middle of a forest. The white pine had been delivered and set up that afternoon. As with everything, her parents liked to make tree decorating an event. Wendy sighed. She enjoyed the holidays, too, but sometimes her parents' frivolity was too much. Maybe she could sneak away and go back to the station, peruse old files for story ideas.

A wet nose pressed into the palm of her hand and she looked down, surprised to see the stray. "Where have you been, Rover? I thought you went home, but here you are." She leaned forward and scratched behind both of his ears. "Did you meet my parents? Or are you hiding out, like me?"

Oliver trotted in and jumped into her lap. He gave three short yips. "So you're the Jingle Bell dog. I see you two have met."

"Wendy, where are you?" Her father's voice boomed from the kitchen. "We have company."

Wendy groaned. Bernie and Babs liked, no, they loved to socialize. On the rare occasions they were home, the couple often had at least two, if not twenty, people over. Bernie had even become friends with Pierre who owned the computer shop next to The Wildflower. Babs had co-taught a photography class for adults with the high school art teacher, Carolyn Hoffman. Often, professors from the university would stop by. Lifting the dog's floppy, black ear, she whispered, "I'll make an appearance and when they're not looking, disappear upstairs. You, my friend, are on your own." Rover swiped at her chin with a pink tongue. "Sorry, but it's every man, woman and dog for themselves."

Placing Oliver on the rug in front of the fire, Wendy pushed herself up and walked to the archway leading into the hall. She looked back. Both dogs had curled up on the rug, nose to tail. "Chicken." Two tails thumped in harmony. She continued on and into the kitchen, where the carols jangled from a small speaker on the counter, the latest in technology. "Hi, every—" The word died in her throat. Their company wasn't Pierre and his smart wife, Jessica, nor Carolyn and her funny husband, Sonny. Wendy leaned against the counter for support. Their company was Josh Hunter.

"Hi, Wendy." Josh moved from one foot to the other, shoving his hands into his coat pockets and then taking them out again. "I brought—"

"You two know each other. I should've guessed." Babs Valentine raced across the kitchen and reached for Josh's coat. Peeking over their visitor's shoulder, Babs wiggled her eyebrows at Wendy.

Josh threw Wendy a look of concern. "I wasn't planning on staying." He shrugged his jacket back up over his shoulders.

"Nonsense. We need a guinea pig. Wendy, take this boy into the dining room and set the table with the holiday dishes. This is a trial run for our party next Saturday." Bernie pulled a crystal punch bowl from under the counter.

"And he's tall. He can put the angel on top of the tree. You're saved from bringing in the ladder, Bernie." Babs reached again for Josh's coat, and this time succeeded in pulling the coat halfway off.

"Hallelujah," Bernie shouted, and then proceeded to sing along with the chorus of the current Christmas carol playing on the radio.

With a glance first at Wendy and then at the woman pulling at his sleeves, Josh finally gave in and allowed Wendy's mother to have his coat. "I can't stay long."

Wendy had seen the panic on his face as
her mother continued to tug at his jacket.
Her heart sank at the thought of Josh having to deal with her eccentric parents.
What must he think? Her father with
his belly and curly white hair could pass
for Santa Claus any day of the year. Her
mother, whose hair had once been as dark
as Wendy's, was now almost snow-white
as well. With her plump, pink cheeks she
could pass for Mrs. Claus. "Mom, Dad, did
you hear? Josh can't stay long."

Babs shoved the heavy jacket into
Wendy's arms. "Hang this in the closet,
dear, then set the long table. The holiday
dishes, like I said." She scurried back to
her husband's side. "Ready for the eggnog,
Bernie?"

"Ready as I'll ever be, sweetie." Bernie
set the crystal punch bowl at the end of
the oak table and propped his hands on his
hips. "Do you remember where we got this
punch bowl?"

"It was a wedding present from the vice
president at your old firm, remember?
What was his name? Harvey? Harry?"

Wendy caught Josh's eye and motioned

toward the hall. They left her parents trying to remember who had given them the fancy punch bowl.

"Heinrich!" Her father's declaration followed them.

"I'm sorry, Josh." Wendy opened the closet door and stuffed his jacket inside. She moved on to the dining room, looking for the holiday dishes. She found the set on the bottom shelf of the antique sideboard. "My parents sometimes get overly excited and think everyone feels the same way." Only then did she hazard a glimpse at the man who had followed her without saying a word. "Just have a cup of eggnog and then slip out. That's what I'm doing."

With a nervous smile, Josh took her hands in his. "Listen, I'm sorry for how we left things last time. I was unbearably rude."

"You had every right. I seem to have trouble determining personal space when it comes to stories. I'm sorry I interfered." She handed him four plates.

He gave her a smile that warmed her heart. Things were back on track. "Dining room or den?"

Wendy grinned. "You catch on quick." She pulled four stemmed glasses, decorated with holly, from the shelf. "The long table's in the den to one side of the archway."

No sooner had they set the glasses and plates on the table than Bernie appeared with a crystal punch bowl of white froth. Babs had followed with a matching ladle. "I'll let you do the honors, honey bunny."

"Nonsense, Babs. We'll let our special guest have the first taste." He handed Josh a cup of creamy liquid. "My special recipe."

Josh leaned down and sniffed the concoction. "I smell nutmeg. What else?"

"Eggnog. With ice cream. And that's all I'm going to say. Secret recipe and all." The man elbowed his wife, and they shared a chuckle.

Wendy approached Josh. The small cut-glass cup looked like a toy in his big hands. "I have to warn you, Dad's eggnog is extremely high calorie."

Babs eyed Josh up and down as he went to stand next to Bernie by the fireplace. "Seems like this fella can use a few extra pounds, Wendy." Her mom's eyebrows once again wiggled.

Fighting growing irritation, Wendy lowered her voice. "Would you stop that?"

With a knowing look, her mother handed her a cup. "I thought you liked the preppy type."

Wendy glanced across the room, where her father was urging Josh to harmonize on a Christmas carol. "You know, Mom, this one kind of took me by surprise."

HEAD SWIMMING, JOSH sat in his truck outside the Valentine home. Lights blazed from the windows. Lighted icicles hung from the porch eves. Bernie and Babs certainly knew how to have fun. Brad and Sue could take lessons from the couple.

Josh had been careful to accept only one glass of chardonnay, the wine Bernie chose to accompany the crab puff hors d'oeuvres. Ice cream had been his downfall. By the time he saw the two empty bottles of rum on the kitchen counter and realized they were in the almost empty punch bowl, it was too late. Josh had indulged heavily. The alcohol had taken its good ole time showing up in his system. But here he was, about to drive home.

Starting the truck, he pulled slowly down the long drive until he was about to pull onto Last Chance Road.

He didn't have far to go. And it was unlikely anyone would be driving here this time of night, and even less likely anyone would be out walking. But he had made that assumption once before and lived to regret it. He killed the lights and shut off the truck. Maybe if he walked around, breathed in the cold, crisp air.

Getting out of the truck, he looked up at the sky. Stars blanketed the darkness. Closing the truck door with a soft click, he wandered toward the road, searching for constellations. The Valentines were nice people, although he understood Wendy's comment. They were uncommonly attuned to one another. But they were also a lot of fun. He hadn't laughed so much in years.

He was leaning against the front of the truck, staring up at the night when he heard a twig snap. His thoughts went immediately to the mountain lion he had seen in Montana. His ears pricked. His father had said there were plenty of coyote and bobcats in Pennsylvania. But it was a tail-wagging Rover who came around the corner of his truck.

He sighed in relief. "Hey, boy, what are you doing out here?" He crouched and ruffled the dog's ears.

"We could ask you the same thing." Like a ghost, Wendy appeared out of the darkness.

Josh's breath caught in his throat. She looked lovely in a bright red coat with a white scarf wrapped around her neck, her dark hair, as always, framing her cheeks. He hoped she couldn't see the red creeping up his neck. He was embarrassed to be found hanging out at the end of her driveway. He stayed crouched, petted the dog, buying time. "There's no moon tonight. I was looking at the constellations. They're so bright."

Wendy tilted her head back and looked at the sky. "Not a cloud in the sky." Rubbing the back of her neck as she returned her gaze to Josh and the dog, she grimaced. "Hard on the neck though."

Josh hesitated only a moment. Even

though Wendy had discovered him, he still wasn't ready to drive back to the cabin. "Follow me." Retrieving his sleeping bag and pillow, he lowered the tailgate and spread the bag in the bed of the truck. "How's this?"

Wendy came around and studied his arrangement, then lowered her gaze to the high tailgate. "I don't think I can—"

Before she completed her sentence, Josh had wrapped his hands around her waist and lifted her. He caught her startled gaze for just a second before hopping up beside her. He lay back, rested his head on one side of the pillow, his legs dangling off the end of the truck. "I'll share my pillow with you. Easier to see the stars."

Wendy appeared to weigh his offer, then finally lowered herself to the cushioned surface and rested her head next to his. "You're right. This is better."

They lay in silence for only a minute before Rover jumped into the bed and lay down at their heads.

"He sure has made himself at home, hasn't he?" Josh felt comfortable, content.

And he had a beautiful woman at his side. What more could a man want?

"I can't help but think someone is missing him." Wendy raised her arm and pointed to an area just above the pine trees lining the drive. "Look, Orion the Hunter."

"It's so dark you can make out almost everything. There's Sirius, the Dog Star."

"Do you know light pollution prevents eighty percent of the people living in North America from seeing the Milky Way? We're really lucky."

Josh reflected on her comment. Lucky? Yes. At this moment he felt lucky. She was waiting for a response, but he couldn't give her that one. "Yes, the stars are certainly beautiful tonight."

"Some people have never seen the sky like this. I guess I can understand why my parents retired here."

"Then why are you in such a hurry to leave?" The question, which was none of his business, was out before he realized.

"Because I haven't been anywhere yet. I want to experience different locations, different cultures." He felt her turn her head on the pillow and size him up. "You've been everywhere. Why are you in such a hurry to leave?"

"Different reasons, I guess." Josh wished he could explain to her how part of his punishment was avoiding home. But he couldn't help think that while she might be sympathetic toward him, she would see a story. "Your dad really liked your sister's apartment, didn't he?" The man had spent a large part of the evening describing the proximity to popular spots in New York.

"Who wouldn't? Her place overlooks Central Park."

The change in subject achieved his goal. At the mention of her father and sister, Wendy had turned away and redirected her attention to the sky. Josh heard the note of derision in her tone and remembered when she had referred to her sister as her dad's favorite daughter. "You know, your dad loves you." Somehow the darkness made it easier to talk of love, something he wouldn't normally have done.

"Oh, sure he does. Just not as much as Katie. Katie is the golden girl, in looks as well as deeds." A sigh sounded from the pillow. "She's been offered a new show, something to do with crime, police work, I don't know."

"What about your interview with Kowalsky? Did it air yet?"

Another long sigh. "Walt said no. He said that since the man wasn't charged, there was no story."

"But he left town, or so everyone thinks. That makes him look guilty." Too late. Josh realized he had done exactly the same thing. He had left Bear Meadows. And even though the man was alive, Josh had changed his life and his wife's life for the worse. He thought of the restored boat. The weights newly cleaned.

Propping herself on one elbow, Wendy sat up to look at him. "You know, I have a motto, courtesy of the woman I hired to find me the perfect job."

"Walk softly and carry a big stick?"

"Very funny. No men, no kids, not even a pet."

"I see. That explains the look of horror on your face when Rover showed up at the door."

She laughed. "Maybe it's time I changed my expectations."

He could no longer see the stars over-head, just Wendy's shining dark eyes. At one time she had said she didn't have time for a boyfriend. Was she making time now? He reached up and tucked a dark strand of hair behind her ear. She was wearing dia-mond studs, winking like the stars above. "You should only change your expectations if that's what you want."

Wendy leaned closer. Her lips were only a breath away from his. Even now he could see traces of her red lipstick she must have worn for her last on-air report. "Why did you kiss me on Thanksgiving, when we went into the kitchen?"

He grinned. "Why wouldn't I want to kiss a beautiful woman?"

She tapped his chest with one finger. "Tell me the truth, Joshua Hunter."

His heart skipped a beat. "You made the best of a bad situation, Wendy. My parents made the dinner so uncomfortable, and you kept trying to make things better. I appreci-ated your effort." He reached for her hand and threaded their fingers together. "I'm glad you were there."

"And the kiss?"

He searched for the right words. "A thank-you."

She squeezed his hand. "Kiss me again, Joshua Hunter."

She was reacting to her parents' tales of their city adventures with her sister, the star, and to the disappointment of her boss refusing to air her interview with Joe. Was she taking a step back from the gung-ho reporter in search of a big story? Because if she was, then maybe she was no longer a threat. Maybe Josh didn't have to be in such a hurry to leave town. And he had told his father. The secret was no longer entirely his. In other words…maybe things could work out. He could stay a few weeks longer, maybe through Christmas, and finish the boat. Hank would definitely get a better price if the boat was finished.

"Hey, Wendy?"

She responded by squeezing his hand again.

"What are you doing next Saturday night?"

CHAPTER FIFTEEN

WENDY HAD JUST finished the Tuesday morning weather segment when Walt asked to see her. Back to her original schedule of early morning and late evening, she had made arrangements to meet Katie, who was driving in from the city, at The Wildflower later. Now, sitting in Walt's office, watching him chew on an unlit cigar, she wondered how dry tobacco leaves could possibly taste good.

"Joe Kowalsky wants an interview."

"He's back? You're kidding." Wendy sat up. The news that the tea shop owner was in town was the last thing she'd expected to hear from her boss. "Why aren't you sending Casey? You said I should stick to the weather. Remember?"

"Yeah, I remember. But Mr. Kowalsky specifically asked for you."

"I suppose he wants the interview Sunday afternoon."

Walt leaned back in his chair and clasped his hands behind his head. "Actually, he's opening his shop today and thought you might stop in. You can do the six o'clock weather from out front. Good segue. Mark wants to do the late night slot."

And of course, whatever Mark wants, Mark gets.

Driving back to Bear Meadows, Wendy wondered if Joe would bring up the last interview. Reopening the shop was a bold move. She pulled into an empty parking spot in front of the coffee shop. Her sister's expensive sports car was already there. She trotted up the steps and opened the door to The Wildflower. The bell rang overhead, and she was hit with the aroma of fresh-roasted coffee beans.

Her gaze was drawn to the crowd in the seating area. In one of the four big chairs sat her sister, dressed in dark jeans and a dark green cowl-neck sweater. Even in casual clothes, her sister gave off an air of sophistication, which wasn't lost on the men perched nearby. Sonny Hoffman, his father, Fritz, Bill and Moose Williams were all leaning forward, elbows on knees, as if they didn't want to miss a word her sister said. Wendy walked over to the counter. No one had noticed her entrance.

Behind the counter, Louise and Holly chuckled over the men's fascination with Katie. Deb, arms crossed, said, "She's like a magnet. A blond magnet."

"A man magnet." Louise ran her red-tipped nails through her blond curls. "You know if I were ten inches taller, I could pull off that look."

Holly fixed the front of her apron, fingering a dried milk splash just below the embroidered flower. "How does she do it?"

"I've been telling you for years. Makeup and better clothes." Louise patted her friend on the back. The bell over the door dinged as Mrs. Hershberger entered. Glancing at the sitting area, she immediately approached the group of women at the counter. "What's going on?"

Wendy hesitated. "My sister is here."

Vera's gray eyes grew wide as she turned and took in the group on the other side of the room. "Katie Valentine is here?" She tapped Wendy's arm and waited until she had her attention. "Can you introduce me?" She beamed.

Wendy was taken aback. This was the most animated she'd seen the teacher since she'd gotten to know her better. What did it matter if she introduced them? She had nothing to lose, and if it brightened the older woman's day, well, that was a good thing. "Sure."

Josh stood at the front window of The Cookie Jar considering who in town would be driving a sports car in the middle of winter. Though the streets were dry, snow and slush lingered in the parking areas and along the curb. His big truck dwarfed the tiny vehicle.

When he saw Wendy pull into the space on the other side of the little red car, all curiosity about the vehicle vanished. His heart quickened as he watched Wendy mount the steps to the coffee shop, her dark hair perfectly in place as always. The night they looked at the stars he had been slightly drunk and asked her out on a date. Later, when the potent eggnog had worn off, he'd driven back to his dad's, wondering if he'd made a mistake. How could he be looking forward to a date and regretting the impulse at the same time?

Across the street a light clicked on, casting a glow through the darkened tea shop. The former banker had returned. The Closed sign still hung in the window.

"Your friend is back."

He heard the oven door slam shut in the kitchen. With a glance at the cookie jar clock on the wall, Josh rounded the counter and stood in the doorway between the shop and the kitchen. "Did you hear me?" A tray of just-iced pastries was on the table. He sneaked one and took a bite. Since coming home, he couldn't seem to get enough of his mother's cooking.

His mother shut off the mixer and turned. She wiped a floured hand across her forehead, leaving a smudge of flour. "Did you say something?"

"Your friend is back." He watched the puzzled look in her light blue eyes fade as she caught his meaning. She went back to the mixer and scraped the sides of the bowl with a spatula.

"Did I ever tell you how we met?"

Immersed in enjoying the textures and sweetness of the pastry, Josh tried to avoid the question. Was now the time to talk to his mother about leaving town? "No." The truthful answer.

His mom stopped her batter making and leaned back against the counter, her eyes soft in memory. "Joe renovated the library into Tea for You himself. The windows were covered in newspaper so nobody, except maybe Deb, knew what was going on. Being the mayor, she always knows. I certainly didn't. I was keeping to myself mostly. One day I went upstairs to change into a short-sleeve shirt because I was so warm from all the baking, and I looked out the window and saw a man going after my rosebushes with hedge clippers." She straightened. Her eyes grew wide at the memory.

"Which rosebushes?" Josh stood and, bringing the coffeepot to the table, refilled both their cups. Then he sat to finish the rest of his pastry.

"Well, they're not my rosebushes." His mom shrugged. "I kind of adopted them.

The librarian didn't want anything to do with them. They line the fence between the library and the park, and nobody was taking care of them. They're heritage tea roses, like my mother used to have. Do you remember Grandma's house?"

"Vaguely."

"I'm kind of glad you weren't around for what I did next. I walked out into the middle of the street and started yelling at him to get away from my rosebushes. By the time I was done, everybody in the coffee shop was out on the porch. Mac walked me back into the bakery. He kind of defused the situation." She chuckled. "I thought he was going to arrest me for disturbing the peace."

Josh reached across the table and took his mother's hand. "We all do something crazy at one time or another."

"Well, I wish I had timed my crazy when The Wildflower wasn't full of customers." She rolled her eyes and then squeezed his hand. "Joe never said a word about my tirade. He just kept bringing me tea samples and making me lunch. You know, I wasn't eating much back in those days."

Josh thought of the box of chamomile tea at the cabin. Just how close had his mother and the tea shop owner been? "You're going across the street, aren't you?"

She nodded. "I didn't even give the man a chance to explain."

"Does this mean you and Dad—?"

"I got the divorce papers Friday." Setting her cup next to the coffeemaker, she returned to the mixer. She poured the batter into a long cake pan and scraped the sides before setting the bowl in the sink.

The sweetness from the pastry was gone. Josh stood and walked to the back door. It looked out onto an alley. The brown cat, the one his mother had called Mister Cee, stared up at him. "It's over then. No hope of reconciliation."

"I'm sorry, Josh. It doesn't mean we both don't still love you. We do."

"I know." He had failed. Again.

"I'll put the cake in the oven. If I'm not back in forty minutes, can you take it out for me?"

Without turning from the door, Josh nodded. "Sure."

His mom bustled about the kitchen, putting things away or in the sink. He figured she was heading for the front door when he called to her, "Don't rush into anything, okay?"

He followed her out onto the porch and watched her walk into the tea shop. Through the glass he saw the two embrace. He felt odd watching and turned away. Four doors down the door to The Wildflower opened, spilling laughter out onto the porch. He turned to enter the bakery.

"Josh?" He stiffened. *Wendy*. Relationships didn't work in his family, so what was he doing asking the reporter out on a date? He fixed a smile on his face, but when he greeted her, he saw she was followed by a tall blonde. The air left his lungs, taking the smile with it. Wendy's older sister, the famous television newscaster. Instead of waiting, he waved and opened the door to the bakery, intending to escape.

"Josh, wait." Wendy smiled tentatively as she approached. Her sister followed more slowly as she took in the sights around her. Wendy's sister didn't miss anything. But when they came face-to-face, Josh could almost feel the woman's full attention. This must be how she attracted the important interviews. He backed up a step. "Hi, Wendy, how are you?"

"I'm good, thanks. This is my sister, Katie. Man, you've practically met my whole family." Her eyes danced and she wore a big smile, obviously happy to be introducing her sister. "What are you up to?"

"I was talking to my mom." He glanced across the street, where both his mom and Joe could be seen, still standing by the checkout counter.

"I hear Mr. Kowalsky is back." When Josh tore his gaze from the couple inside Tea for You and concentrated on Wendy, she motioned to her sister. "Katie, this is Josh Hunter."

Long fingers, neat, white-tipped nails. Her grip was strong. "Pleased to meet you, Josh. I understand you helped my sister out of a snowdrift a few weeks ago. That was kind of you."

He couldn't miss the fact that Katie's eyes were sharp. Those eyes missed nothing. "No problem." This was the newswoman about to start a new television series, something about crime.

"I wanted to talk to you about Saturday." Wendy smiled.

He could see the similarity between the two women. They had the same complexion, a healthy glow and the same shape of face, oval. Maybe since her sister was home, Wendy was canceling, which would probably be for the best. "Okay. Something come up?"

"I just wondered if you could pick me up at the station."

Suddenly chilled, Josh rubbed his hands together and wondered what he had been thinking asking a news reporter out on a date. But he was committed. "Sure."

"Great. See you Saturday." And with a warm grin and a wave the two sisters left.

Looking at his own vehicle, covered with slush from driving along back roads, he realized he had a lot to do before heading west on Interstate 80. A wash, an oil change and a full tank of gas would be a good start.

JOSH HAD FALLEN under her sister's spell just like every other man in town. Yet, instead of wanting to hear her stories, he had withdrawn. When she'd asked him to pick her up at the station, Wendy had the distinct feeling he was having second thoughts. But here they were, sharing a large pizza with everything on it at a cute restaurant in Shadow Falls. And he seemed himself again.

"Are you sure you don't mind? This place has the best pizza around, but it's not very fancy." Josh pointed at the plastic checked tablecloths and paper napkins. Sitting in a red vinyl booth, Josh gave Wendy an apologetic smile.

Trying to break off a long string of mozzarella, Wendy lifted her slice of pizza high in the air. Although her mouth was full, she shook her head. "Um-um." The string broke and stuck to her chin. She reached for her napkin, but Josh beat her to it. When he dabbed at her face, she felt the heat rush into her cheeks. "Except I'm making a mess of things."

"You're enjoying your food. I'm glad." He propped his arms on the table and watched her eat.

"How did you find this place?" she asked.

"It's been here since I was a kid. I spent

some time in Italy when I was in the service. This is the closest I've ever come to Italian pizza in the States."

"No kidding? I'd love to go to Italy someday."

"I'm sure you will."

She returned his smile. If she couldn't even get out of Bear Meadows, how in the world would she ever get to Italy? With Katie home, Wendy's lack of advancement was even more obvious. But she was on a date. For one night, surely Wendy could forget about her career. "Christmas is a little over a week away. Are you ready?"

Josh's eyes widened, and his mouth dropped open. He looked like a little boy who had forgotten to do his homework. "What?"

"Don't tell me you forgot about Christmas."

Josh drew his hand across his face in what was by now becoming a familiar gesture whenever he was at a loss. "I sure did. Of course—" he reached across the table and linked his fingers with hers "—I didn't plan to be home this long." He looked down at their connected hands. "Do you know you have sauce on your fingers?" He got another napkin and cleaned her hand and then his.

"Sorry." She grinned. "I told you I like to enjoy my food."

"Enjoy being the operative word. You didn't say *wear* your food."

"Whatever." She grinned again and tossed the last bite of crust in her mouth. She leaned her head against the back of the booth and closed her eyes. "Oh my, that was the best pizza I've ever eaten."

She was still savoring the rich sauce when, glancing down at their entwined fingers, Wendy felt an unaccustomed warmth. She lowered her voice. "You're taking care of me again."

His lips curved up, but he just shrugged as he released his hold and tossed the soiled napkin on the empty pizza tray. "Are you in a hurry to get home?"

"Are you kidding? Katie's there. What did you have in mind?"

"I thought I'd take the scenic route back to Bear Meadows."

Wendy didn't bother to tell Josh it was

dark out and they wouldn't see much. "Sounds just fine, Mr. Hunter."

They were driving along a back road bordered on both sides by tall trees when the truck began to sputter and cough.

Josh shifted to a lower gear. "Uh-oh."

In the lights from the dash she could see his look of concern. "Something wrong with your truck?"

"Not exactly." Josh gave her a sideways glance that seemed slightly guilty.

"Because this truck is brand-new." At her words the truck sputtered and the engine died. Except for the pinging of the engine as it cooled, they sat in silence and, when Josh shut off the headlights, complete darkness. "Should we call a tow truck?"

"No."

"If your truck is broken, then we need a tow truck."

"It's not broken."

She weighed his words. He was being oddly reticent. He loved his truck, and she couldn't imagine his not keeping up with repairs. Then the realization hit her. "Are we out of gas?" In the dimness of the truck cab, she could make out Josh nodding. She punched him in the shoulder. "You forgot to put gas in your truck? What the heck, Hunter?"

He dropped his forehead onto the steering wheel. "I meant to fill up when I got the oil changed. I had laundry in the washer and I forgot." He lifted his head and reached for her hand. "I'm sorry, Wendy."

He looked so dejected Wendy couldn't help but laugh. "You've had a lot going on. I hope you know where we are. Can we walk the rest of the way?"

"There's good news and bad news."

"Oh, brother. Give me the bad news first."

"We're seven or eight miles from your house."

"And the good news?"

"We're only a mile from the Smith farm. We should be able to get gas from them."

Once their eyes adjusted to the darkness, Josh turned off his light and they walked down the country road hand in hand, aided by the meager glow of a quarter moon. Hiking the long driveway to the Smith house, they were glad to see a light on in a downstairs window.

They were greeted by Hawkeye. He wore a faded plaid housecoat, flannel pajamas and worn leather slippers. Opening the door wide, he ushered them inside as if he were accustomed to getting midnight visitors. "Gas? There's a full can in the shed out back. Wait here while I go get it."

But Josh insisted on retrieving the can, and Wendy waited in the living room with Hawkeye while Josh disappeared outside. She looked around the old-fashioned living room. Portraits of ancestors hung on flowered wallpaper. Yet a big-screen television took up most of one wall. The half-finished pieces of wood scattered on the coffee table reminded her of the twins' internet business. She looked up and caught her host watching her. "How's your business going?"

"Good." He leaned back against the couch and crossed his legs. His slipper dangled from his foot.

Wendy sighed and wondered if even her talented sister could pull words from the reticent farmer. She tried again. "Would you be interested in some free advertising? I work for WSHF, you know."

"I'm familiar with your work, Miss Valentine."

Wendy squirmed on the sofa. So that's how it was going to be. People in this town had long memories. She was glad to hear the door open and close.

"Ready to go?" Josh appeared in the doorway.

Wendy jumped up. "Of course." She turned back to her host. "Nice talking to you, Mr. Smith."

He nodded and followed them both to the door. He rested a hand on Josh's shoulder. "Take care of yourself, son. You need anything else, just let me know. I'll be up for a while." Then he turned his gaze on Wendy, and she felt herself shrinking under his knowing eyes. "Miss Valentine, it's been a pleasure. You take it easy on this young man, you hear?"

When the door closed behind them, Josh shot her a look. "What was that about?"

She shrugged and took his hand. "Who knows?"

Thirty minutes later they pulled around to the back door of the Valentine home.

Except for a light in the kitchen, the house was dark. Josh shut off the truck.

"Do you have enough gas to get home, or will I find you at the end of the driveway tomorrow morning?" Wendy tugged at Josh's coat, teasing.

He reached for her hand and held it in a tight grip. "You're funny, you know that?" He moved across the seat toward her.

Her heart rate increased. She pressed her hands against his chest. "Are you sure you didn't run out of gas on purpose?"

Josh leaned in and pressed his lips against hers. When he pulled away, his voice was low. "I'll never tell." He held her in his arms, and they sat for a long moment in the darkness. She wondered if Josh was still planning on leaving.

"I just had a great idea," she said.

Josh smiled and tucked a strand of hair behind her ear. She liked it when he did that. "What's that, Ms. Valentine?"

"I spent Thanksgiving with your family. Why don't you spend Christmas with mine?"

Josh pulled further away. His eyes grew guarded.

"I figured since both families are eccentric in their own ways, you'd be okay with that." She waited, but he didn't respond. "Is my family too weird for you?"

Shaking his head, Josh dropped his chin to his chest. "Your family is great, Wendy. It's me. You don't want me at a family dinner. Believe me."

She searched his face. "That's ridiculous, Josh, I do want—"

And before she could utter another word he covered her mouth with his, and all thoughts of why he had again put up his guard left her head. Yet this kiss was different. This kiss had an air of desperation. She had heard about goodbye kisses. Looking into the face of the man she had met in the middle of a blizzard, she realized she was falling in love with him. She also came to another realization. This kiss had a message attached. This kiss said goodbye.

CHAPTER SIXTEEN

JOSH WATCHED HIS mother roll out the bread dough, but his thoughts were on the evening before. The walk in the woods with Wendy. Holding her in his arms. He had lost his mind.

"I'm closing the bakery."

His mother's words pulled him from his memories. He must have misunderstood. "What did you say?"

"Joe is buying Dr. Reed's mansion. You can see the place from the back door of his shop, so it makes sense, and, of course, he's keeping Tea for You open. He offered me the kitchen to bake in." She flipped the dough, and a cloud of white flour enveloped her. "So I won't need this space anymore."

"He's staying in town?" She could have knocked him over with a feather. "Deb Gold won't be happy losing your rent."

"She already has new occupants lined up."

"Mom, you promised you wouldn't move fast. Your divorce just became final."

"Your father and I have been separated for a while, Josh. I'm tired of living in a storage room." She punched the dough with her fist.

"You're moving in with him?" His voice rose at the end. He was worried for his mom.

She paused, her knuckles pressing into the puffy white mixture. "He offered me the apartment above the garage."

Josh sat down heavily. At her mention of the garage, everything came flooding back. Sneaking Dr. Reed's scotch, borrowing the car, the night on Last Chance Road when he thought he had hit a deer.

"Josh, what's the matter? You're as white as the flour on this board." She dropped the mound of dough in a large bowl and covered it with a towel. She set it aside and leaned back against the counter, arms crossed.

Josh rose and walked over to the back door. Mister Cee was nowhere to be seen. He jerked when his mother's hand gripped his shoulder and squeezed. "This arrangement with Joe…it's strictly business. I got married when I was eighteen. I want to stand on my own two feet for a while."

"What about the mortgage fraud. Are you sure you can trust the man?"

"He went back to Pittsburgh to close up his house and put it on the market. He had forgotten his mother used a voice-activated recorder in the music room. He and Vanessa were in that room when she warned him he was going down with her."

Josh was stunned at the news. "Can it be allowed as evidence in court if the person doesn't know they're being recorded?"

"You forget. Joe was never charged. But the tape clears his name. Anyway, there's no doubt she was setting him up to take the fall. He didn't know anything about what she was up to. The bank even offered him his job back."

"And I suppose he refused." Josh's concerns were weakening.

"He said he likes living in Bear Meadows. It's a fresh start for him. Either way, he doesn't want to live in Pittsburgh anymore."

"Well, that clinches it, then." Josh bent down, and, grasping his mother by both shoulders, kissed her on the cheek. "Time for me to move on."

"Oh, no. Can't you stay for Christmas?" She cupped his face. "Please, Josh?"

He knew he should leave town. Another cabin called to him. The one in the mountains of Montana. "I'll think about it, Mom. But no promises."

"I'LL JUST OPERATE the camera."

Zipping up her boots, Wendy shot her sister a look. Outside, the sun peeked through heavy clouds. Snow had fallen overnight. "But surely you must have other things to do. What are Mom and Dad up to?"

Katie grabbed her black wool coat and winked. "I'll be quiet as a mouse." Twenty minutes later Wendy sat on Vera Hershberger's overstuffed couch and wished she had told her sister no. "Thanks for taking the time to see me again."

"Where were we when we left off last time, Wendy?" Vera asked, her gaze falling on the camera set up at one end of the living room. "Why don't you come sit down, Katie?"

Katie shook her head. She wore her honey-colored tresses loose today, making her look even younger than usual. "Just pretend I'm not even here."

Wendy bit the inside of her cheek. *When had that ever happened?* "We were talking about your interest in science and your trip last year."

Vera, clearly delighted, clapped her hands. "That's right. It was a fabulous trip, all thanks to my students."

"Any favorites? Students, that is."

Vera leaned back in her chair, her eyes on the photos on the piano. "Oh, I suppose. But all the children had something special about them."

"Do you see them often?"

"A lot of them leave the area and don't get back too frequently. Now Josh, he first left eight years ago, I believe, because it was right after Hank's accident that he graduated. He was supposed to go to college, but that didn't work out so he joined the military. He had such promise. It's always hard to see a good student not reach their potential."

"Which class—"

"What happened to Hank?" Katie's clear voice interrupted.

Irritation prickled her nerves. Wendy had wanted to ask that but didn't feel comfortable about it, given her recent track record with interviews. Katie obviously had no problem asking the hard questions.

Vera sat forward and directed her response to Katie. "Hank and I used to go for a walk after supper, almost every evening. We liked to keep in shape." She glanced down at her figure and smoothed her shirt. She wore a sweatshirt with a red cardinal on a snow-covered holly bough. "We used to, I mean." She grew silent. Wendy exchanged a glance with her sister, who mouthed *sorry* and motioned for her to continue.

"So you and Hank were on a walk?" Wendy prompted.

"That's just it. We normally walked together, but I had papers to grade. By the time I told Hank I couldn't go, it was later than usual. Darker too." She looked down at her shirt again, running a finger over the snow. "So you might say the accident was my fault. He left the house, and at Last Chance Road, it was completely dark. And those trees along that road make things even darker." She shook her head.

Wendy sat back in alarm. "He was hit on Last Chance Road? That's where I, where we, live."

"Yes, I know, but this was before your parents built their house. The only people living on that road was the family at Last Chance Farm. I'm not sure if anyone's living on that property anymore."

Wendy was still processing the fact that the accident had happened so close to her home. She didn't realize how much time had passed until she heard her sister ask the retired teacher the next logical question.

"Who hit him?"

Wendy glanced at her sister. Of course, the ultimate professional could continue the interview no matter what kind of revelation had come out. Then she looked at the woman.

"We never found the driver. It was a hit-and-run," Vera said.

"SHE LOOKS GOOD." Hank wheeled slowly around the boat. His eyes reflected his excitement, and a smile stretched from ear to ear. He looked nothing like the man who had greeted Josh the day he brought over the sandwiches and cookies. "Never thought I'd see this finished. You did a good job, son."

Josh ran a hand over the glossy paint. "I wouldn't have known what to do without your direction. So I'd say it was a team effort."

Hank stopped at the stern. "Maybe when spring comes you can put her in the water, see how she operates."

Which was the one thing he absolutely couldn't do. He couldn't stay in Bear Meadows until spring. He thought about the conversation with his mother. There was really no more reason to stay in town, Christmas or no. Wendy or no.

The weight bench sat in the corner. Josh walked over and picked up a five-pound dumbbell. Then he carried it over to the man in the chair and placed it in Hank's right hand. "Tell you what, Mr. H. I'll see what I can do about getting the boat in the

water if you try out some of these weights."
An empty promise, he knew. But if the man
started working out, maybe he would keep
going after Josh left.

Hank closed his fingers around the
weight and automatically flexed his arm.
"Oh, so you're bribing me, are ya? You
must be taking direction from my wife,
too." He lowered and raised the weight a
few times before dropping it into his lap.
"But what's the point?"

Josh straightened. "What's the point of
anything, Hank? Maybe if you get strong
enough, you can lift yourself in and out of
the boat."

"Aw, I doubt it." But Hank's eyes as they
moved over the hull and up to the wheel-
house brightened and the smile almost
returned. He ran a finger along the red
trim and took a deep breath. "Let's go in
the kitchen and see if we can find some
snacks."

The sun glared off the new snow as they
left the garage. The temperature had gone
up at least ten degrees. The ramp was covered in wet snow. "Hold on, Hank, let me
sweep off the ramp." He got a broom from

the porch, and when he finished, he went around to the back of the wheelchair to push Hank up the ramp. He heard the door open and the teacher's greeting but his attention was on the chair as he helped Hank maneuver forward. When they were both safely on the porch, Josh finally looked up, expecting to see Hank's wife. His heart stopped when he recognized the other women with Mrs. Hershberger.

Katie Valentine held a video camera to her shoulder. Josh could see the green light, indicating the camera was filming. He turned away and looked out over the small yard. His breath came in short gasps.

She knew. Wendy's smart sister. The famous reporter.

She knew.

CHAPTER SEVENTEEN

"I THOUGHT YOU liked the preppy type." She and Katie were on their way back to their house. And they still hadn't finished the interview. Once Hank returned from the garage, Vera had, with a shake of her head, indicated they would have to continue it later.

"What makes you think I like him?"

Katie chuckled. "I could light a fire from the sparks I've seen between you two. Although today he was acting kind of weird."

"Your imagination is getting away from you, sis. He didn't stick around long enough for you to make any assumptions. Funny he didn't come in the house, though."

"I think I spooked him. Most people want to be on television—" she poked her sister in the ribs "—unless they've got something to hide. How well do you know this guy?"

"I know he's a veteran. He was a medic in the army."

"A medic. Hmm. Something seems off about him. I'd be careful if I were you. Besides, didn't Ms. King tell you to avoid entanglements?"

Wendy no sooner pulled up to the back door than her father appeared. He motioned to them to hurry inside, raising his voice so they could hear him. "You're just in time for cocktails, girls. We found a new recipe with bourbon and apple cider."

Wendy glanced across the seat to her sister. "Do you mind if I…"

"You're leaving me alone with these two?" Katie gave her a knowing smile. "Don't be too long, okay?" She shut the car door behind her and said a few words to their father. With a wave and a smile for Wendy, her sister followed him into the kitchen.

Just before the door closed, the black dog slipped through and wandered down the steps.

Wendy sat behind the steering wheel. Josh's odd behavior had her curiosity aroused. She opened the passenger door.

"Come on, Rover. Maybe you can help me figure out what's going on with Josh."

The dog climbed onto the seat just vacated by her sister. "Don't tell anybody you rode in the front seat, okay?" In response the dog lay down and rested his chin on the console. She put the car in Drive and headed back down the drive to Last Chance Road.

Wendy steered slowly around the frozen ruts in the lane leading to the cabin. Josh's truck was parked in the usual spot. She turned off the car and sat there, wondering what to say. Finally, she opened the door, waited until the dog exited and then ran up to the porch. She knocked, but with the temperature dropping and knowing he was there, she entered the cabin, Rover right behind her. The fireplace and the hearth had been swept clean. The table and countertops were bare, except for the overturned coffeepot. And no sign of Josh.

She walked over to the mantel. Even the matches were gone. She turned and looked up at the loft. A railing had been added. It extended down the stairs, which had also been finished. She walked slowly up the stairs. Her head had just cleared the landing, and she saw Josh kneeling by the window that looked out over the stream.

"The railing looks nice." When he didn't respond, she continued until she stood on the top step. "What are you doing?"

"What does it look like I'm doing?"

The tone in his voice took her by surprise. "Uh, the cabin is clean, your duffel bag is packed. I'd say you're getting ready to leave."

He turned from the window. The hurt look in his eyes frightened her. "Such a smart girl." He stood, but remained stooped over until he got past the rafters. "I tried to avoid you. But you just kept showing up in the oddest places. And you're pretty, too." He propped his hands on his hips. "You're the total package, Ms. Valentine." He gave her a sad grin before brushing past her and clomping down the stairs.

When she saw he was headed for the open door, she hurried after him. "Are you upset my sister got you on film? I'm sorry, Josh, she does that all the time." She caught up to him and reached for his arm. When he faced her, she recoiled at the fear she saw in him.

"I knew I shouldn't get involved with you. My bad. You brought in the big guns. I may not be as smart as you and your older sis, but I get the picture."

"What are you talking about?"

"I confess. There, is that what you want to hear?" He slapped his face in mock horror. "Oh no, you forgot to set up your camera. Wait, maybe you have one of those hidden cameras. Where is it? In your lapel?"

"Stop it, Josh." She stepped back. She didn't even recognize the man in front of her.

Josh leaned down and whispered, "This *is* what you're after, Miss Hotshot Reporter. I committed a crime eight years ago. A hit-and-run, never solved, until you and your older sis joined forces and came to town. Tell me, does your sister have a spot for you on her new show?"

Josh's words seemed to bounce around in her head like Ping-Pong balls. *A hit-and-run?* The only hit-and-run she knew about was... She lifted her hand to her mouth as realization dawned. "No, you couldn't have. You were planning on becoming a physical therapist. You wanted to help people."

Josh bent down and ran a hand over Rover's head, sending his tail wagging back and forth. "Goodbye, fella." He looked up and held her gaze for just a moment before turning away. "Lock the door when you leave."

The truck door slammed, the engine roared to life and then the sound of wheels on gravel. And then nothing.

She looked at the dog who stood in the doorway watching Josh leave. "I don't understand, Rover. Why was he spending time with Hank if he was the one who put him in the wheelchair? He couldn't be the one. He just can't." She walked over to the open door and stared across the lane to the creek flowing past. But then she remembered the times she'd tried to refill his glass and he always put his hand over the top.

Or the time he had too much of her father's eggnog and parked at the end of her drive. And when Mrs. Hershberger said the words *Last Chance Road*, the thought had flicked into her brain, but just as quickly disappeared. *Secret number three*.

When she heard Josh's truck returning, her heart jumped for joy. He was coming back. He was coming back to explain. But when she saw the old farm truck pull into sight her hopes fell. She shut the cabin door behind her and settled onto the swing. Rover raced down the steps to greet the newcomer.

The truck door screeched as Hawkeye got out of the truck. He knelt on one knee. "Hey, there, Buddy, where have you been?" The dog raced around the older man, alternately sitting and rolling over before trotting around in circles. Rover seemed happier than usual upon seeing a stranger.

"He's happy to see you. Do you know this dog?"

Hawkeye grinned. "The chief and his missus gave him to me couple years ago after my hound died. This is Buddy, Junior. I wondered where he'd got to."

Wendy watched man and dog get reacquainted. *Buddy?* "He's your dog?" She pushed off with a foot and set the swing moving back and forth. The happy dog pushed his nose into Hawkeye's hand. "I kept asking who had lost a dog around here. Didn't you tell anybody Buddy was missing?" *What was wrong with the old man? Why would he intentionally allow her to get attached and then—*

"Nope. Buddy here is half coonhound. Those dogs travel for miles when they're on a mission. I figured he'd come back when he was done doin' whatever he was doin'." Hawkeye grinned. "Josh around?"

Her throat tight, all she could do was shake her head. Hawkeye ambled over and eased his lanky frame onto the top porch step with a sigh. "Gone for good, is he?"

Still swinging, she nodded. "Whatever happened to Betty?"

The dog sat patiently, his head resting in the old farmer's lap. "She's back in California." Hawkeye scratched behind the dog's ear. The dog's tail thumped on the wood porch floor. "With her family."

"With your family."

The man shrugged. The dog caught sight of a squirrel and scampered off. "Josh go back to Montana?"

Wendy tried to catch the man's eye, but

he was watching Buddy race around the tree the squirrel had climbed. "Do you know where he stays in Montana?"

Hawkeye returned his attention to Wendy and nodded. "He stays with an army buddy. We were talking about friends made in the army, how some of them are friends for life." He stood, rubbed his right knee and started for the truck.

Getting information from the man wasn't an easy task, but she wasn't about to give up now. "What's his friend's name?"

"Come on, Buddy. Let's go home." Jumping over the side of the truck, the dog landed with a thump in the truck bed. Hawkeye opened the driver's door and paused a minute before giving her a long, solemn look. "Josh has trouble letting go of his heart. You might want to keep that in mind."

She stood. The swing bumped the back of her legs. "What's his friend's name, Mr. Smith?"

"MacDougal. Matt MacDougal. His uncle owns a large working ranch outside of Great Falls." Hawkeye got in the truck and with a loud screech slammed the door.

Backing out of the front yard, he pulled away. Buddy's paws rested on the tailgate. The dog was smiling. Of course he was. Buddy obviously loved the man.

She wasn't exactly sure what she should do next. The man was gone. The dog was gone. Not even a kid in a fictional minivan. But her news reporter status was back. *No men. No kids. Not even a pet.* Katherine King would be pleased.

Also, Josh was right about one thing. His story fit perfectly into Katie's upcoming news show. Small town. Unsolved crime. And she was the only one who knew.

CHAPTER EIGHTEEN

"COME ON IN." Matt greeted Josh at the door of the main house and motioned down the hall. "I was just reading the paper in the den."

"Thanks." Josh closed the door, hung his parka on the coat tree. In the den, a fire blazed in the huge stone fireplace. A newspaper lay open on a footstool. He settled into the chair opposite. He had driven straight through from Pennsylvania. His bones ached and his eyes burned. No questions, no *why are you here a week before Christmas?* Just *come on in.*

"Aunt Steff and Uncle Ernie went into town this morning. Snake and I fed the horses, and I thought I'd catch up on the news." Folding up the paper, he laid it to one side and propped stocking feet on the stool. Crossing his arms, he threw a casual glance Josh's way. "How was your trip east?"

Josh leaned forward and propped his elbows on his knees. A plush rug lay at his feet. "I've got good news and bad news." He gave his friend a weak smile. "Which do you want to hear first?"

"Your choice, my friend."

"The good news is my mother isn't sick. She lost about forty pounds because she wasn't eating due to stress."

Matt rested against his chair, his arms still crossed. "That's good, right? So long as she's dealt with the stress."

"Right. I thought she had cancer or something."

"And the bad news?"

"My parents got divorced while I was home."

"Aw, man, I'm sorry." Matt paused before continuing. "That explains you showing up here now."

Josh stared down at the carpet of deep blues and red swirls. "Not entirely." At one time, he thought he could tell Matt anything. The two had been through a lot together. If his friend knew the kind of man

Josh really was, would he still have welcomed him into his uncle's house? "I have something to tell you. If, at the end, you want me to leave, I'll understand."

So he told Matt the whole story. The argument with his father, borrowing the car and hitting what he thought was a deer. When he was finished, they sat in silence. The logs in the fireplace snapped and popped, sending sparks up the chimney like fireworks. Finally, Matt broke the silence. "Why don't we take your things upstairs?"

Josh looked up from the bright carpet to his friend's face. "Excuse me?"

Matt stood and poked the fire before turning back to Josh. "You can stay in the spare bedroom. We have lots of room." He headed toward the hallway.

Josh had expected more questions. *Why didn't you go to the police when you realized what you had done? Why did you wait so long to tell anyone?* Instead his friend offered him a place to stay. He shook his head. He didn't deserve Matt's friendship.

Matt's voice came from the staircase. "Are you coming?"

Josh hurried into the entry and looked up at Matt, leaning against the banister. "What should I do?"

Matt gestured to him. "Look, you know I've always got your back, but you have a decision to make. I can't help you."

Suddenly anxious to be alone, Josh grabbed his parka from the coat tree. "I'd rather not stay here. I thought I'd stay at the cabin."

Matt frowned. "The temperature's dropped twenty degrees since you were here, Josh. That cabin's hard to heat."

"I'll be fine."

Matt ambled back down the stairs. "You'll have to ride Blue up the mountain. The pickup's out of commission." No more questions, as if he understood that sometimes a person just needed to be alone.

"What happened?" He hadn't expected the ranch truck to be unavailable. After driving twenty hours straight, the last thing he wanted to do was ride a horse.

"Snake drove it into a ravine right after you left. It's still there."

Josh shared a smile with Matt. Snake was great with horses, but terrible with anything mechanical. "Maybe I should take my truck. I'm not great with horses."

"You don't want to scratch your new truck. Besides, Blue's bombproof."

So here he was, riding the blue roan gelding up the narrow, rock-strewed road to the cabin. Blue was as sedate as Matt had promised. When they flushed a grouse, the roan just pricked his ears and plodded on.

Josh was able to keep busy for a while, unsaddling the horse, turning him into the corral and then taking his duffel bag into the cabin. He put away the food supplies Matt had insisted he take, then started a fire. When he reached into his pocket, he withdrew the pink pack of matches. He opened them. Three matches left. He held the flame to a crumpled up newspaper and then dropped the pack on the mantel.

He heated a can of stew over the fire and wiped out the bowl with a piece of buttered bread. Darkness had fallen on his first night back, and, thanks to the nonstop drive from Pennsylvania, he fell asleep quickly. He was grateful. But the next morning he stared at the rafters. Josh searched his brain for ways to occupy himself.

There wasn't much to do this time of
year, but Josh felt he had to do something
to earn his keep. He repaired part of the
corral that had fallen down. He cut and
stacked more firewood. The week dragged.

FRIDAY MORNING WENDY was first in line
at the Shadow Falls Regional Airport for
standby. The ticket agent, a shaggy-haired
middle-aged man with a dark beard gave
her a lazy smile. "Two days before Christmas, huh? Lot of people traveling, you
know."

Wendy scanned the crowded termi-
nal before leaning close and lowering her
voice. "I have to see someone. We left
things kind of, well, messy." The ticket
agent, whose name tag read Al, smiled for
a minute and then tapped his fingers on
the keyboard. "If you go through Atlanta, I
might be able to book you via Dallas, then
Denver, and then Great Falls. You'll get in
this afternoon, assuming you don't run into
any hiccups. They're calling for snow out
west, you know."

"Thank you so much—" of course she
knew they were calling for snow out west

"—Al." *Atlanta*. How poetic. At one time she thought Atlanta was a destination. Now it was just a stopover.

"Happy to be of service." He worked some kind of magic because she got the last seat on the first flight out. In Denver she sprinted between terminals and actually got on an earlier flight than scheduled. When she got into Great Falls Airport she rented an SUV because the man told her if she was going into the mountains she would need it. After all, they were calling for snow.

The openness of the plains amazed her. The mountain ranges were jaw-dropping. The drive in to the MacDougal ranch was ten miles long. She saw Josh's truck as soon as she came in view of the house. She parked, approached the home and knocked on the door.

"Yes?" A tall woman with neat salt-and-pepper-colored hair answered the door. A man's flannel shirt hung from her shoulders. Her jeans were worn. "Can I help you?"

"My name is Wendy Valentine and I'm looking for Josh."

"You better come in, dear. It's so cold out." She opened the door wide and stepped back. Wendy entered and spotted a staircase that led up to the second floor. A chandelier made of antlers hung from the ceiling. "Come into the den. We have a nice fire going."

She followed the woman into a bright, inviting room with smart features and comfortable furniture. She chose the plaid sofa, and the woman, a matching chair.

"Now, you're here to see Josh, you say?"

"Yes, ma'am."

"Call me Steff. I'm Matt's aunt. How do you know Josh?"

"I... I'm from Bear Meadows, Pennsylvania. Like him."

"I see." Steff looked at her hard. "Are you the reason that young man is hiding in the mountains?"

"Excuse me?"

"I haven't seen him since he got back. I thought he was reclusive before..." Her forehead creased with worry.

"So he's not here?"

"Matt said that as soon as he'd arrived,

he saddled up Blue and took him to the upper cabin."

Wendy slumped in her seat. "Oh no."

Steff offered a warm smile. "You're welcome to stay until Matt and his uncle get home. Matt can take you up in the truck."

"When will they be here?" Hope sprang to life in her chest.

"Tomorrow. They went to get some equipment."

And hope just as quickly died. "So a vehicle can get up there then?"

"It's not the easiest to navigate, Wendy. That's why Josh leaves his brand-new truck in our garage. We only take the older four-wheel drive vehicles up on the mountain."

"The rental agent told me the SUV I rented could go off road."

Steff stood and walked over to the window as if trying to come to a decision. Then she turned. "You better wear my parka, dear. We're expecting snow. And you best leave now. Put that rental car in low gear and just crawl up the road. Okay? Watch out for the deep ruts. You don't want to get hung up." Shaking her head, Steff muttered as she headed for the hallway. "I hope I don't regret this."

HE HAD WOKEN to an ominous sky. Dark clouds hung low over the treetops, making Josh wish he had taken Matt up on his offer and accompanied him and his uncle to Helena.

He'd thought he wanted solitude. Five days seemed to be his limit. He peered up at the overcast sky and wondered what was next on his to-do list. Keeping busy was the only way to crowd out the thoughts of regret.

He doubted Matt and his uncle had dropped the rest of those dead trees along the fence line.

Matt had asked him to wait, so they could do it together. But by the time Matt would return, there could be a foot of snow on the ground. Felling the trees wouldn't take long. He could ride Blue to the site, fell the trees away from the fence and be back by lunchtime.

As Blue picked his way down the rocky slope, Josh almost understood Matt's preference for a horse over a truck in the mountains. Except for the scrape of the gelding's hooves and the occasional screeching of the hawks, silence reigned. Though the clouds hung low, he could still see the roof of the ranch house and the long lane leading out to the road.

He had to come to a decision. He couldn't hide in these mountains for the rest of his life, expecting the MacDougals to support him when all he did was fix fence. He knew almost nothing about horses and even less about cattle. He was of little use to the family.

Blue's sudden jerk to one side sent his heart racing as he fought to maintain his seat in the saddle. "Whoa, there, boy. If you were trying to wake me up, it worked." He looked around, searching for what had spooked the old gelding. To his left a mass of pines blocked his view. To his right he could see the fence line through the bare trees. "Just a little bit farther, fella."

The words were no sooner out of his mouth than the horse jerked. Josh grabbed for the saddle horn as he listed to one side. He caught a glimpse of tawny fur as Blue reared. His hand slipped from the saddle horn as he fell backward. When his shoulder impacted a fallen log, pain shot through his arm. A hind hoof grazed his leg as the horse struggled for purchase on the slick ground and whirled to race back up the slope.

The mountain lion crouched between the fallen trees. Then the long, sinewy body disappeared into the pines so quickly Josh was no longer sure what he had seen. He tried to lift himself out of where he was wedged, but the pain forced him back to the ground. He lay against the wet ground. Snow drifted down from above. Then everything faded to black.

AUNT STEFF TRIED hard to convince Wendy to wait until Matt and Ernie had returned home. In the end, Matt's aunt had provided her with her own heavy boots, socks and parka. The rental agent hadn't lied. Following Steff's advice, she kept the vehicle in low gear and the SUV crept steadily up the hill, jouncing from one rut to the other but never stalling out. When she finally made it to the cabin, she breathed a sigh of relief. She hoped Josh appreciated her effort.

She parked directly in front of the cabin, slamming the door when she got out. Then she waited for Josh to come see who his visitor was.

A horse stood, head down, in the corral. Josh Hunter was home. Steff told her he had ridden a horse up the mountain rather than risk scratching his truck. She turned in a slow circle. The man couldn't have picked a better place for reflection. The only sign of civilization was the green roof of the ranch house far below. Otherwise all she saw were mountains and trees in the distance.

She looked up, expecting to see smoke curling out of the chimney on such a cold day. But not even a wisp. Maybe he went for a hike.

Leaving her things in the car, she tapped on the cabin door, then opened it. "Josh?" She walked inside. She recognized the duffel bag tossed in the corner. The bedcovers lay just where he must have thrown them after waking. She sat on the bed and asked herself, "Where have you gone, Joshua Hunter?"

She went back outside. She was alone.

More alone than she had ever been. Yet she wasn't afraid. She had a mission, and no amount of wide open spaces was going to keep her from her duty, which was finding Joshua Hunter and telling him exactly what she thought.

Looking for clues, for something out of place, her reporter's instincts kicked in. Her gaze lit again on the saddled horse standing in the middle of the corral. This time she noticed the gate was open.

The hit-and-run wasn't Josh's only lie. He was no cowboy.

Josh had been thrown from his horse. She walked around the clearing looking for a direction. When she found the deep imprints made by the running horse, she started down the rock-strewed mountain.

CHAPTER NINETEEN

"Josh?"

He opened his eyes. Directly above him a squirrel sat on a branch, chattering and clasping a nut in his tiny paws. Overhead, the clouds were barely visible in the dark sky. How long had he been out? Cold seeped through his body. He closed his eyes.

"Josh?"

He was dreaming. He thought he heard Wendy calling his name. Wendy. He had thrown away the best woman he'd ever met.

"Josh." Something brushed his cheek, caressed his forehead. "Wake up."

He opened his eyes to Wendy's beautiful face framed by raven hair. He wasn't dreaming. He was hallucinating. But when she tugged on his arm the pain was a reminder he was still alive and Wendy was real. He moaned. "I think it's broken."

"Oh, my goodness, Josh, you have to help me. Your skin is like ice. We've got to get you on your feet." Her hand caressed his face.

He reveled in the warmth. "Let me just lay here a minute." The fog pulled him back closer to the damp ground.

"You have to get up. It'll be completely dark soon."

Twigs snapped. Leaves rustled. He remembered. "Cat." His throat was dry and his tongue thick. "Wendy, there's a cat. Somewhere."

"No cat, Josh." She had gone around behind him and pressed on his back with her shoulder. "Push against me and try to stand. I bet your legs are okay."

His eyes popped open at the spasm of pain that shot through his midsection. At the same time he swept his gaze along the stretch of pines for the big cat. His thigh muscles strained as he came to a standing position. He dropped his chin to his chest as a wave of dizziness swept over him.

"Don't fall, Josh, please don't fall."

He shuddered as she wrapped an arm

around his waist. "Ribs. My ribs might be broken."

"Okay, take it easy." She released the tight grip around his chest and held on to his belt. "Let's see if we can make it to the cabin."

"Cat, Wendy." He couldn't tell if the words were in his head or on his lips. All he could do was warn her. "Cat, Wendy."

THEY WERE BOTH soaking wet and dirty when they got to the cabin. She could barely see in the darkness. Every step had brought a grunt of pain from Josh's lips, though she tried to be careful where she supported him.

Once they'd entered the cabin, Wendy eased him onto the bed and immediately lit the lantern. What to do next? She thought back to when he had rescued her from the snowdrift. He had been afraid of hypothermia. The first thing he did was start a fire. But she had waited dry and warm in a heated truck. His wet clothes had to go. She pulled off his boots, then replaced the wet clothes with a dry shirt, sweatpants and socks from the duffel bag. She'd have to get that fire going soon. Then she covered him with a blanket. "You've been wanting to do that to me since you met me." His speech was slurred.

She smiled, pleased he was conscious, until she had a thought. When Josh had brought her in from the cold, he said her speech was slurred and he feared she was suffering from exposure. Seeing his sleeping bag next to his duffel bag, she unrolled it and laid it over top of him. She ran a hand over his face, his stubble rough against her fingers. His eyes were closed. They needed a fire now.

A pack of matches lay at the edge of the smoke-stained mantel. *Sue and Brad.* Gold script on a pink background. Had he kept the matches on purpose? Or did he just want to use them up to erase the bad memories? She got the fire going, grateful for the stack of wood piled in the cabin. She set a basin of water on the hearth to heat, and with a last look at Josh, went outside to retrieve her suitcase.

Snow fell like a silent white curtain from above. She looked over at the still-saddled horse in the middle of the corral. "I'll be right back to take care of you, fella."

She changed into dry clothes, checked on the basin of water by the fire. With a quick look at Josh, she went outside and moved the horse into the small barn, removing his saddle, finding hay and breaking the ice in a water bucket.

The water in the basin was ready by the time she returned. Dipping a washcloth in the warm water, she knelt by the bed. "Josh? Should I let you sleep?"

She wiped the dirt from his face, only then seeing the scratches from when he had fallen. But he didn't move. "Josh, what do I do? You're the medic." She rinsed out the cloth and washed each of his cuts. Then she covered him up again.

Tea. He had woken her and given her tea. She checked the cabin, peeking in drawers and cupboards. No tea. She found a box of instant hot chocolate mix.

So she added a packet of hot chocolate mix to a fresh cup of warm water and stirred. Instead of a frothy mix the powder stayed in clumps. She gave the cup one more stir and carried it over to the cot where she perched on the edge. "Josh, wake up." Getting no response she set the cup on the floor and patted his face. "Josh."

He stirred. His eyes were just slits, but he smiled. "Hi, sweetie."

"You need to drink something warm. Can you sit up?" He bent forward but groaned in pain. "Stop. Let's try something different." She tucked another pillow behind his head and held the cup to his lips.

He slurped. A drop ran down his chin. She wiped it with the wet cloth. "Hmm, that's good, honey." Another smile.

Wendy smiled. "It's lumpy warm chocolate. How long were you out there anyway?" She startled at the thought she didn't know when he had last eaten. "Are you hungry?" She looked back at the drawers and cupboards.

"No food. Not now." He lay back against the pillow and closed his eyes. "I hurt."

"I know. What should I do?"

She was about to move away when he whispered. "Stay."

She touched his face. "I'll be right back."

"Lay next to me." His plea came out in a whisper. "Please, Wendy."

"I don't want to hurt you." Minutes later, she slipped under the blankets and lay down next to him. She shifted onto her side and rested her arm across his middle. "Does that hurt?"

"No." Another whisper. His hand moved slowly until his fingers covered hers. She listened to his breathing. The only light in the room came from the fireplace. She was thinking about the wisdom of allowing Josh to sleep, when he spoke.

"Remember the first night we spent like this?" His breath tickled her chin.

"Yes. For a lot of it, I didn't even know your name."

His laugh turned to a groan. "You know what?"

"What?" She pressed her hand to his cheek, which still felt cold, and tucked the blanket tight around him.

"I wasn't asleep." His eyes fluttered, then stayed open, searching her face for a response.

"Hi, there, blue eyes. Welcome back." She ran her thumb over his lower lip. "You know what? I wasn't asleep, either."

He started to take a deep breath, but grimaced halfway through. "I'm messed up, Wendy."

"I know. Your ribs and your arms. I'll get us back down the mountain as soon as it's daylight. Can I do anything else for you? Should I splint your arm or something?"

"Just lay here with me." One corner of his mouth curved up. His eyes fluttered again until he was staring up at the ceiling. "I'm messed up in my head, Wendy."

She knew what he was referring to. His secret. The one he thought she and Katie had figured out. But now wasn't the time. "No you're not. You might have a concussion, but you're lucid. You have some broken bones." She studied the man next to her. "You're going to be fine."

"Remember the night we looked at the stars? You and Rover showed up while I was waiting to get sober." He twisted his neck until he could look at her. "By the way, what did you do with Rover?"

"I haven't had a chance to tell you." She propped herself on an elbow so he didn't have to strain to see her. "Rover belongs to Hawkeye. His name is Buddy."

"No kidding. Wasn't Hawkeye worried about him?"

"That was the strange part. He wasn't surprised at all to find Rover staying with me. He acted like Rover, I mean, Buddy, was on a mission. That Hawkeye, he's a character." She took a breath, smoothing the wrinkles in the blankets. "You were talking about that night we looked at the stars."

"Orion is my middle name. I guess my mom thought it appropriate with my last name being Hunter."

"Joshua Orion Hunter. I like that. It has a ring to it." She smiled at him warmly.

"Anyway, the night we looked at the stars."

She remained propped above him, waiting for him to explain. "What about that night?"

"That's when I knew I was falling in love with you."

Her heart skipped a beat, then another. "I love you, too, Joshua Orion Hunter."

HIS BODY FELT like it had been put through a wood chipper. He groaned.

"You're awake." Wendy appeared in his line of vision. How did she always manage to look like she had just stepped out of the beauty parlor? "Merry Christmas. Today is Christmas Eve."

"When did you get here?"

"Yesterday. I found you in the woods, remember? You fell off the horse."

"I didn't fall off. I got thrown. Bomb-proof. Yeah, right."

"When I found you, you kept saying 'cat.'"

"I need a drink." Josh tried to lift himself off the bed but the pain was too great. "Help me up."

She propped him up and found support for his back. "There, how's that?"

"Good. Now, please, get me a drink."

Her forehead creased, but she disappeared and then returned with a cup, which she held to his lips. "Easy."

He sputtered and turned his head away. "Not water. There's a bottle in the cupboard." She looked puzzled but went over to the cupboard as he asked. He lay back against the pillow and tried to recall the previous day.

"This is scotch, Josh. Do you want coffee? I could make some."

He raised his voice. "A drink, Wendy. Pour the scotch in the cup and bring me a drink."

"You're kidding, right? It's seven in the morning. And I'm no medical professional, but I doubt you're supposed to have alcohol when you're hurt. You might have internal bleeding or something."

"I'm the one who got thrown off the horse."

She didn't answer. She returned with a cup and held it to his lips.

"Hot chocolate? Where did that come from?" The question brought to mind the image of Hank Hershberger in his wheelchair, bitter and angry. How poetic that Josh was now an invalid.

Her beautiful lips were pressed in a thin line. "I'm not giving you alcohol. I don't have to be a medic to know that's a bad idea."

"Go away. I don't want you here."

"You're being ridiculous." She went to the cabin door and opened it. "I'd drive us down the mountain, but the snow looks too deep. I'm sure Matt will be here soon."

"What difference does it make? I mean, what does it matter if I drink? I'm not driving." He laughed an ugly laugh. "I'm not even riding a horse. I'm just staying out of everybody's way up here on top of the mountain. If I want to drink—" he threw the cup across the room "—then I'll damn well drink." He tried to rise, but bit back a cry of pain and sank onto the bed.

She went over to him then. "What about last night?" She reached for his hand. "You told me you loved me, Josh."

"Love? You want to talk about love?" His voice came from a place deep within him that he didn't recognize. "You haven't even asked me if I plan to turn myself in. Come on, you must be curious how my sordid story plays out." He paused. "There's no happy ending, Wendy." When she didn't respond, he twisted the knife a little further. "But then, you're not a fan of happy endings are you? Happy endings don't make for a good story."

CHAPTER TWENTY

MATT, ERNIE AND SNAKE showed up mid-morning in the heavy-duty pickup with the plow attached. They had plowed on the way up so Wendy's vehicle could get back down the mountain. They loaded Josh in the back of her SUV, Matt drove, claiming his experience driving the road would save them time. Wendy sat in the back, trying to keep Josh from getting bounced around too much. They stopped for only a moment when they got to the ranch to let Ernie out, and then Wendy and Matt drove Josh to the hospital.

"Are you family?" The clerk at the registration desk looked at Wendy over half-moon glasses.

She shook her head. "Just a friend." *And barely even that*, she wanted to add. "His family is back in Pennsylvania."

"Then we'll see how things go. In the

meantime, fill out what you can of this form."

"Can I go with him?"

The clerk eyed her up and down, and then nodded. "He looks pretty banged up. He could probably use the moral support, honey."

She finished the forms and then wandered down the hospital corridor, peeking behind curtained alcoves.

Matt appeared from the farthest alcove, speaking to someone. "I said he was bombproof, not cat proof."

Again with the cat. Wendy touched his arm to get his attention. "How is he?"

"They're taking him to X-ray. Come down to the cafeteria with me, would you? I'm starved."

With a last look toward Josh's room, Wendy accompanied Matt to the cafeteria. When they were seated, he gave her a look. "Do you know about Josh?"

"What do you mean?"

Matt lifted the top slice off his sandwich and looked around. "Be right back." He returned with ketchup and added a dollop on top. He took a large bite and studied her as he chewed.

Wendy fiddled with her tea. Each time she looked up he was still watching her, chewing methodically. "Do you mean Josh now or Josh...before?"

Matt swallowed and, avoiding her gaze, inspected his sandwich. "Before."

"How long have you known?" she asked.

"He just told me."

"He assumed I'd figured it out. Ha. He gives me more credit than I deserve. He went on a rant just before he left Bear Meadows and pretty much admitted everything. I was shocked."

"Me, too." Matt finished his sandwich, his drink and carried the dirty dishes to the counter. When he returned, he sat back down.

"We should be with him, don't you think?"

"I just have one more question for you."

Something in the way he said the words caused Wendy to press back against her chair. The phrase *dynamite comes in small packages* came to Wendy's mind when she met his gaze. "You can ask me anything."

"Are you putting his story on your sister's news show?"

AFTER BEING POKED and prodded and wheeled around to multiple departments, Josh was returned to a semiprivate room on the third floor. Luckily, the adjacent bed was empty.

"What's the verdict?" Matt entered the room, followed by Wendy. "Although your arm in a cast tells me a lot."

"That's the bad news." Josh grinned. "The good news is they finally gave me some painkillers." He stole a glance at Wendy, who seemed more interested in the show on the television hanging on the wall than his diagnosis. "Cracked ribs and a slight concussion. I guess my head bounced off one of those logs. Broken arm. Oh, and exposure from laying on the ground all day. Other than that, I'm just dandy."

Matt perched at the foot of the bed. "You always were a tough one. Heck of a way to spend Christmas." Josh's gaze remained on Wendy, who stood with her back to the two men. "I'm guessing they want to keep you a few days."

Josh nodded. He couldn't seem to take his eyes off Wendy. But then, he shouldn't be surprised. He had been hard on her that morning.

"Tell you what, fella. I'm going to head home. We'll come back early in the morning to check on you. Aunt Steff will want to bring you a goody package." He stood. "I'll leave you two alone. Wendy, when you're ready to go back to the house, I'll be waiting down in the lobby."

She gave Matt a bright smile. "That won't be necessary, Matt. I can get a cab to the airport." When she finally met Josh's gaze, the smiled disappeared. "I'd like to be with my family for Christmas." When she walked over to the bed, he thought for a moment she would kiss him goodbye. Instead, she pried open his fingers and dropped a dark blue button onto his palm. His loose shirt button from the day after they met. "Goodbye, Joshua Hunter."

WENDY SAT ALONE in the den staring into the fire. Her sister had picked her up at the airport at noon. The day before, she had gotten as far as Denver. The last plane to Atlanta had developed mechanical problems, so she'd spent Christmas Eve in the

Denver airport, watching the snow fall outside. Wendy had then discovered that Christmas Day was the perfect time to fly. The airports were practically deserted.

From her spot in front of the fire, she could hear her parents laughing in the kitchen, preparing dinner. Even Oliver, the Yorkshire terrier, had made himself scarce, as if he knew she wanted to be alone. The lights were lit on the tree.

"Why are you sitting in here in the dark?" Her father switched on a lamp by the couch. He sat down across from her. "It's snowing again. You made it home just in time."

"You and Mom need any help in the kitchen? Is Katie helping?" She knew they didn't. They never did. They were a self-contained unit, needing nothing but each other. But she couldn't think of anything else to say.

"Katie's upstairs on her phone and your mother's icing the Yule log." He chuckled. "Maybe this year she can roll up the cake without breaking it in two. Remember last year's log? It was fifty percent icing. It took so much to hold it—"

A minute passed before she realized he had stopped talking. She glanced up and smiled. "You couldn't tell by looking at it. And it still tasted good."

Her father nodded. "Want to talk about it?"

She shifted in the chair and pulled her feet under her. "There's no point, Dad."

"Is this about that man you went to see in Montana, or the Miami job?"

Wendy had been sitting outside Harrisburg International Airport, waiting for Katie to arrive, when her phone had rung. She had half expected the caller to be Josh. But instead the caller was Katherine King, wanting an answer on the Miami anchor position. She had said yes.

"You know I'll never be Katie, don't you, Dad?"

His eyebrows shot up. "What are you talking about?"

"You were always boasting about Katie to your friends, how she anchored a national news desk at twenty five, how she knows famous people, that she has a fabulous apartment overlooking Central Park." She bit down on her lower lip. "That's not me, Dad."

Her father leaned forward, put his hand

on hers. "I don't expect you to follow Katie's footsteps, although I thought that's what you wanted. I just want you to be you."

"I wanted to see the same look in your eyes when you look at me that I see when you look at Katie."

Her father shook his head. "When I look at Katie, I see a little girl whose mother deserted her, deserted both of us. Until Babs came along, it was the two of us. I guess I always felt she needed more attention than you did. You had your mother, your real mother. Babs and Katie were close, but not as close as you and your mom, because she had you from birth. So I always thought Katie needed more support, encouragement. I'm sorry if you thought I loved you any less, because I don't. I love both of my girls."

"You don't think less of me because I'm not in New York by now?"

"Your sister is fourteen years ahead of you, don't forget that. Your time will come if it's what you really want. Don't you want to go to Miami?"

"I'm looking forward to it. Kind of."

"Good. I was hoping while you're down

there you can find us a deal on a two-bedroom condo. I hear it's a good time to buy." His face relaxed, his usual contented expression returning.

"You'd really do that for me?" Finding an apartment to rent had been one of the issues weighing on her.

He grinned. "Sure. You can live there, and your mom and I will have a place to stay when we come down in the winter."

"Thanks, Dad. That's a load off my mind."

"Which leaves Josh Hunter."

She nodded.

He leaned back in the leather chair and sighed. "From what I've heard, the man has a lot to come to terms with before he's ready to—"

"—commit. I know." Wendy looked over at her father. His lips were pressed tight together, a rarity for him. That was okay. He had confirmed exactly what she felt in her soul. Before she and Josh had any chance of being together, Josh had to face his demons alone.

THE ONLY LIGHT came from the hallway. The floor was quiet, except for the occasional voice from the nurse's station. Josh slept, but each time he woke his thoughts returned to Wendy. He closed his eyes, only to dream again.

Dr. Reed stood at the foot of his bed.

"You've made a mess of things, haven't you, son?"

"I'm sorry, Doc."

"So what are you going to do about it?"

"It's too late. Did you see Hank? He's been in a wheelchair for eight years."

"What did I always tell you, Josh? Medicine is part science and part miracle."

"Merry Christmas, Josh. How are we feeling today?" The fluorescent light over his bed burned through his eyelids.

Josh struggled out of the depths of a restless sleep. Beside him, a nurse was checking his IV. "You have to work today, huh? That stinks."

"Well, it's Christmas, it's snowing *and* I'm earning double time. Mom's cooking dinner, and I get off at two. I'm a happy camper. What about you? I'll bet you're down because you're missing a big family celebration. Don't worry, they'll probably all show up later to visit you." She paused halfway out the door. "They'll be bringing breakfast soon. Anything else I can get for you?"

"No, thanks." The door swung shut behind her.

Big family celebration? He grunted. *Hardly.*

CHAPTER TWENTY-ONE

A CURLY-HAIRED YOUNG woman dressed in a white lab coat strode into the room. "You ready to go home today?"

Josh looked down at his one arm still in a cast. "I guess."

She peered at her clipboard and scribbled some notes. "You know, you're lucky your girlfriend found you when she did. I hate to think of the condition you'd be in if you'd spent the entire night outdoors." She patted his shoulder and smiled. "You'll need help for a few weeks. You've been staying at the MacDougal ranch, I hear. I met Matt the other day."

"He's a good guy. He's come to my aid more than once." Someday he would pay the MacDougal family back, but he had imposed long enough. He would manage. He always did. He gave the doctor his most charming smile. "So I can get dressed and go?"

"You can, and while you're doing that, I'll write up instructions and give you a couple of prescriptions. I think your family's outside, waiting to see you. Take care, Josh."

"Thanks, Doctor." Josh sat up. The stab of pain in his side reminded him about the broken ribs, but he stayed upright. He kicked at the light blanket covering his legs.

"Quit thrashing around, boy, before you end up on the floor and break something else."

Josh froze at the sound of the familiar voice. "Dad?" His father was standing in the doorway. "What are you doing here?" Then he caught sight of someone else. "Hawkeye?"

"Hello, Josh. Got yourself in a bit of a pickle, I see." The older man glanced around the room.

Unexpectedly Josh's eyes began to burn. He could only blink away the gathering tears. "I'm fine. You didn't need to come all this way."

"Actually, I'm headed for California."

His chin dipped. "Figured it was about time I met my daughter and grandson."

Josh took a breath, as deep as he was able to given the cracked ribs. "That's a huge deal."

Hawkeye nodded. "The time is right for me to make amends."

Josh looked at his father. "Are you here to tell me what a mess I've made of things again?"

Shaking his head, his dad approached. He rested his fingers on the edge of the bed, as if afraid to touch his son. "I thought I could drive your truck back home."

Josh fought the familiar irritation at one of his father's announcements. As usual, his dad spoke in bullet points, assuming the rest of the world knew what he was thinking. "Why would I want you to drive my truck home?"

"Aren't you coming back?" One dark brow lifted, exactly as it always did when he was waiting for an answer.

Josh closed his eyes, but as soon as he did Dr. Reed's ghost appeared. *So what are you going to do about it?* He had made the decision days ago, after he had been thrown and before Wendy found him. He had to make amends, too. He just didn't know how. But here, part of the solution stood before him. He was going home.

CHAPTER TWENTY-TWO

"TOURISTS WERE STUNNED yesterday when an abandoned Jet Ski ran into a man in the waters of Biscayne Bay. Fortunately, the Miami Fire and Rescue team was nearby and took the man to the hospital. No sign of the driver of the watercraft."

Wendy turned to address a different camera. "And finally, on this Monday morning, a reminder that you have six days to find something special for Mom on Mother's Day. Our chief meteorologist, Launa Starr, has the long-range forecast to tell us what kind of weather we can expect on Sunday." She turned to the young woman seated next to her and couldn't hold back her smile. The dark-haired beauty was a bundle of energy, moving around the set with enthusiasm and charm. She had actually convinced Wendy to chase tornadoes with her and the crew just a few months earlier. The second time the meteorologist asked, Wendy had politely declined. Once was enough.

Wendy relaxed for a moment, watching Launa explain the upcoming changes in the local weather. The Miami anchor position had been a good move, no doubt about it. New job, new location, new people. Maybe she'd finally get to travel.

Launa pointed to a screen displaying clear skies. "No storms on the horizon, folks, so if you want to take mom sailing this weekend, it'd be a perfect time."

She didn't think about Josh as much as she used to, either. Maybe only once a day now. She knew from her sister that Josh had come home, confessed to Chief McAndrews, who then went with him to see the Hershbergers. Her sister had featured the unsolved cold case on her new show, but had focused on the human interest element. It was the only way that Hank and Josh would agree to be interviewed. Vera had also gotten in on the act. Wendy chuckled. And here she thought interviewing a small-town teacher was too small potatoes for Katie.

Wendy had watched the broadcast, fascinated at the outcome. The statute of limitations on what had happened that fateful night had run out, but the Hershbergers insisted they wouldn't have wanted Josh charged, anyway. It had been an accident, and that had been that. Katie went back to work in New York, their parents were traveling through the Panama Canal, Walt had returned to Seattle and Wendy had no idea what had happened to everybody else. Did Sue and Brad get together finally? What about Hawkeye and his twin grandchildren? Did he ever meet them? And where did Josh run off to this time?

"You're zoning again, Wendy. Launa's about finished." The soft voice in her ear brought her back to the studio.

"And if you can't find time to shop, or sail, at least take your mom out to dinner. With all the choices we have in South Florida, you can't go wrong. Don't you agree, Wendy?" And the blue-eyed meteorologist beamed a bright smile.

"You are right on the money, Launa. I vote for seafood." Wendy focused on the main camera. "And that's it for us today.

We will see you tomorrow morning. Have a good week, everyone."

JOSH STOOD IN the soundproof booth with the producer of the show. Wendy hadn't changed a bit since she'd left him in Montana. Her hair was as dark and shiny as ever, although she sported a nice tan from the hot sun of southern Florida. For the third time that morning, he wondered if he had been right to leave her alone while he got his life in order. Six months had passed; she could have met someone. Heck, she could've gotten married. He strained to check her left hand, but she had it tilted to one side. "She's not married, is she?" He nudged the shoulder of the man seated at the board.

"Wendy or Launa?"

Josh shot the man a puzzled frown, but, standing behind him, the expression was wasted. "Wendy."

"Are you kidding? She has a motto—"

"I know. *No men, no kids, not even a pet.*" Her style seemed different, though it suited her. She had just a touch of mascara, and the coral lipstick looked perfect with her tan. Even her clothes were more relaxed. No more suit. She wore a yellow dress.

"So what are you doing here?" The producer continued to move switches, still staring straight ahead.

Josh took a deep breath. "Trying to get her to change her motto."

"Well, good luck." He then spoke into the mouthpiece of his headset, "And we're clear."

He and the producer watched as Wendy and the weather reporter laughed about something spread out on the desk in front of them. Wendy unhooked her microphone, stretched and made to leave.

"Wish me luck." Josh exited the booth and waited in the hallway outside the studio. His heart pounded with the anticipation of talking with Wendy after such a long separation.

The door opened. Josh stood face-to-face with the morning anchor of the South Florida television station. "Hello, Wendy."

She froze. To her credit she didn't make a scene. In fact, she didn't do anything at all, except brush past him and continue down the corridor. Josh ran a hand over his face. He knew this wouldn't be easy, but he hadn't expected the news reporter to clam up. He turned in time to see her disappear through a door at the end of the hallway.

The door had her name on it. He knocked and entered slowly. "You're probably wondering why I'm here."

Wendy sat in front of a mirror wiping her face and eyes with a moist towelette. Smudges of mascara appeared on the towel. Leaning closer to the mirror, she appeared satisfied with the results before picking up another bottle and smearing lotion on her face.

Josh noted a desk in one corner was covered with newspapers and a computer. A small television screen hung on the wall. A local talk show was on. Josh noted from the tape that ran along the bottom of the screen the temperature was already 80 degrees and at only nine o'clock in the morning. Josh pulled the desk chair over to the makeup table and sat down. "Just give me thirty minutes. Then, if you want me to leave, I will."

Wendy stood and hung her navy blue

blazer on a hanger and then stepped behind a screen. She still hadn't said a word. Josh looked down, uncertain now as to what to suggest. He had screwed up. He should've come after her as soon as he had straightened things out back in Bear Meadows.

"Thirty minutes."

Josh raised his head. Wendy had changed into white shorts and a sleeveless print blouse. Her face, devoid of makeup, had her looking nothing like the serious professional who had sat at the anchor desk just minutes before. He continued to stare, drinking in the sight of the woman with whom he had fallen hopelessly in love. The slight frown reminded him he had only thirty short minutes. Maybe twenty-nine now.

He jumped up and grabbed her hand, not giving her time to refuse. He detoured to pluck a paper bag from the beverage station before they headed outside. He felt a tug as she tried to free her hand, but he hung on, gesturing to the park next to the bay. "Over here."

The look on Wendy's face wasn't promising.

Josh chose a bench he had scoped out the evening before. The sun was making the water shimmer and sparkle, and there were a few boats just setting off. "I wish I had a skinny vanilla latte for you." Did he see a slight smile?

Wendy leaned back and looked out over the bay.

"I brought cookies, though."

Wendy's gaze slid downward at the bag between them. "Your mom's?"

"Mom's homemade sugar cookies." Reaching into the bag, he pulled one out and presented it to her. "They got a little broken on the trip. I had to stuff them in the saddlebags." He glanced at an old motorcycle parked in the shade of a tree.

"Thank you." She accepted and bit off a tiny bite. "Wait a minute. Saddlebags? Where's your truck?"

He leaned back against the bench, like she had, and finished his cookie. "I sold it."

He said the words so casually, he liked how it sounded. A lot. He'd known it was the right thing to do. "What? Did you just say you sold your vehicle? Why?"

He nodded. "Hank needed a special

truck to pull his boat to the lake, so, with the money I got from my truck, and a little extra, we bought something he can handle. It's pretty neat."

She gave him a long look. "I can't believe you sold your truck. Where'd the motorcycle come from? It seems kind of old."

Josh gestured at the bike under the tree. "Hawkeye gave me his Panhead Harley. He said he and Betty used to take it out on Highway One, but he figured their motorcycle days were behind them. I told him I wasn't sure about that and to let me know if they changed their minds." His words brought a smile to Wendy's face as she finished the cookie.

Josh followed her gaze to the stunning bay. He had everything planned. Step one. Cookies from home. Step two. Explain what he had been doing for six months. "I apologize for how I treated you in Montana. I know you were just trying to help. I wasn't in my right mind."

For the first time, Wendy directed her dark eyes at him and looked him full in the face. She waited a full minute. "Apology accepted." She glanced at her watch. "Eighteen minutes."

He didn't have a second to spare. "Lying in that hospital bed gave me a lot of time to think. I realized no good comes of telling a lie, that one lie just begets another. I couldn't move forward until I went back and made amends. Hawkeye and my dad showed up. My dad rode back with me."

"How's Hawkeye?"

Josh smiled. Wendy still cared about the folks back in Bear Meadows. "He drove on out to California and met his daughter and grandchildren. He's staying out there for a while."

"What about Skinny?"

"He stayed with Joe in the mansion through the winter. Now he's back at the farm." He gave her a look. "As soon as I got home I went to see Mac McAndrews and told him everything."

"I know."

Josh gave her a puzzled look.

"I saw my sister's interview."

"About that... Your sister said you weren't interested in participating."

Wendy shrugged. "I was already working here by then."

Josh reached for her free hand. When he realized he was holding her left hand, he looked down, just to be sure. Her ring finger was bare. "Your sister was fair. I could have been treated much worse by the media and people." He laced his fingers through hers, and, when she didn't resist, he felt the slightest encouragement. "After my cast came off, Hank and I started lifting weights in his garage. For his age, that man is strong."

"So you're free and clear."

"Legally and every other way. The Hershbergers said they believed my remorse for what had happened was genuine. And it is. All they asked is that I go back to school."

"I see." Wendy withdrew her hand and resumed her study of the busy dock area on the other side of the park. "They want you to go to Penn State."

"They want me to go to school. I thought I needed a change of scenery. So I applied to the University of Miami. Wonder of wonders, I was accepted."

At that, Wendy whipped around to face him, her eyes wide. "Here? You want to go to school here?"

Josh recognized the look. It was the same look she'd had when Buddy had shown up on the back porch as a stray. "You know that *no men, no kids, not even a pet* motto works for Ms. King, but maybe it's time you found your own motto."

"Look, Josh, I'm happy for you, but I still don't know where I'm headed. I still want to find my…my niche as a reporter."

Josh held up one finger. "Hold that thought. For once, my timing is good." He ran across the grass, over to the parking lot. Hope flickered in his breast.

A van had pulled up outside the station. The driver opened up the back and said something to Josh. The young man reached in and carefully picked something up. Jogging back across the grass, he set a basket on the bench between them before kneeling in front of Wendy. "I'd arranged a present for you."

Wendy's eyes narrowed, looking from the basket to Josh and back again.

"Go ahead. Undo the latch." Josh rested a hand on her knee.

No sooner did she release the lid than a chubby bundle of black fur leaped onto her lap. Wendy laughed out loud as the Labrador puppy planted her paws on her chest and licked her chin. "Josh, what have you done?"

"Wendy, meet Maggie. Maggie, this is Wendy." Josh leaned back on his heels. He was fairly certain of the reaction the puppy would evoke, but, until now, wasn't 100 percent. But Wendy's wide smile and giggles assured him he had made the right decision.

"Shh. Settle down." Wendy smoothed the puppy's fur until she stretched out on her lap and rested her chin on her big paws. Wendy tilted her head and gave Josh a half grin. "You're not playing fair. Labrador puppies are almost irresistible, but how—"

"You can still find your niche, Wendy. But I want to be part of your adventure." He offered up a teasing smile. "Consider me your on-call dog sitter. Anytime. Although, everyone knows puppies are a chick magnet, so I won't be held responsible if—"

Josh's persuasive words were cut off when Wendy leaned forward and planted a kiss on his lips. Which is what he was hoping for all along.

Maggie yipped three times, then curled up on Wendy's lap. She was home. They all were.

EPILOGUE

Wendy pushed on the thick glass door leading from the television station to the sidewalk outside. She looked across the street. Josh stood by the same bench they had sat on three years earlier when he had come to Florida to plead his case. Maggie chased after a tennis ball.

Wendy had been resistant at first to the idea of keeping the dog, but Josh had convinced her if they took turns caring for the animal it could be done. Lifting her face to the midmorning sun, she closed her eyes and breathed deeply. She could smell the ocean. She had grown to like the smell.

She crossed the street and rounded the bench. "Hi, Maggie." The Lab jumped up and wagged her tail. She rubbed the sweet dog's ears and smiled at Josh. "And hello to you, too."

Josh leaned over and gave her a quick kiss on the lips. "How was the broadcast?"

"Good. My parents texted to say they'll be here any moment. So, are you ready?"

"To graduate? You bet. It's been a struggle at times, but having you by my side made all the difference." He squeezed her hand.

"We managed."

Josh was watching Maggie sprint toward them. "I can't believe your sister is coming to my graduation."

"She's proud of you. We all are." She reached down for the ball and tossed it onto the grass. Maggie ran after it.

The dog returned and dropped the ball at their feet. Maggie stood, tail wagging, looking from one to the other.

"Does this dog ever get tired?" Wendy laughed and threw the ball as hard as she could. "Mom wants to go down the Ocean Highway to Key West while they're here. Want to tag along?"

"Maybe we'll find some key lime ice cream to go with the key lime pie."

"You and your ice cream." Wendy wrapped her arms around his neck and gave him a long, slow kiss. "Here they all come." She watched Josh's face as he stared at the crowd coming from the parking lot.

"I wasn't sure if my dad would come or not." His voice was soft. He sat up straight. "Wait a minute, is that—"

"Hawkeye and Betty." Wendy poked Josh. "You're quite the popular fellow." She smiled as his face reddened. Despite his good grades and his volunteer work with the local veterans group, Josh still had trouble believing in his own worth. Today would go a long way toward showing him his misdeeds were in the past.

Josh now stood, squinting into the glare of the sun. "Who is that walking behind your dad?"

Wendy tingled with excitement for the coming celebration. She waited, anticipating the moment of realization on Josh's face. She wasn't disappointed. His jaw dropped, and his beautiful blue eyes widened. "No, it's impossible," he said.

Wendy stood on her tiptoes and whispered in his ear. "What did Dr. Reed say?"

"He said—" His voice cracked. "He said 'medicine is part science and part miracle.'"

"Well, there you go." She tore her gaze from Josh and smiled as the group approached. Bernie and Babs, Sue and Joe, Brad and Katie, Hawkeye and Betty. They all paused, as if rehearsed, and stepped to one side. Hank and Vera Hershberger walked arm and arm through the grass toward Wendy and Josh. Hank leaned heavily on a cane, but his steps were sure.

"Did you know?" Josh sounded hoarse, his soft words barely spoken.

Wendy nodded. "I sure did."

When the group reached them, Hank extended his hand and took Josh's in his. Josh swiped at the tears in his eyes. He wrapped the man in a bear hug. "How did this happen?"

Hank gave his wife a sidelong glance. "When we started using the boat, I got to thinking what the doctor told me back when all this happened. He said I could walk again. That the effort I put forward was up to me. Your dad offered to drive me to physical therapy, and then afterward we'd pick up Hawkeye and take the boat out."

Josh shared a long look with his father. "I don't know what to say."

"How about, let's eat." Bernie carried a picnic hamper. "Follow me, folks." He led the way to a picnic table near the water.

Josh started to follow when Wendy pulled him to a stop. "Wait, Josh. That's not all."

Josh pressed a hand to his chest. "I don't think I can take anything else."

Wendy slipped an arm around his waist and drew him in close. "About Atlanta in the fall."

He nodded. "I've been submitting applications to physical therapy groups. This is what you've been waiting for. You haven't changed your mind about me coming with you?" He cocked one eyebrow.

"Of course not." She fingered a button on the front of his shirt. "The station offered me a special assignment for the summer. You don't have a job for the summer, right?"

"The one I want isn't available yet. There's a group that specializes in dealing with victims of trauma. One of their therapists is going on maternity leave in the fall. What's this about?" His look of concern was endearing to her.

"They're supplying me with a motor

home so I can travel across the country and interview everyday people. I need a driver." She glanced at Hawkeye and Betty, sitting side by side at the picnic table. She had never seen the man talk as much as he was today. "Starting with twin brothers in Pennsylvania who started a turkey call business in their seventies and became an internet sensation."

"You need a driver and I need a job. Sounds like the perfect combination." He tightened his arms around her and kissed her with passion.

"And something else." She felt a little silly bringing it up, but she wanted to make a point. "Did you know I have a new motto?"

Josh rolled his eyes. "No, and I'm afraid to ask."

"One man, one or more dogs and maybe some kids in the future."

Josh's eyes lit up. "I like it." He nuzzled her neck.

"Okay, you two, break it up. We only have a couple of hours before the ceremony starts. Now eat up." Bernie waved at them to join the others who were eating sandwiches and drinking tea.

"Just a minute, Dad." She turned to Josh. "I finally get to see a little bit of the country, but do you really mind coming with me this summer? Did you want to stay here? Or maybe go back to Bear Meadows?" She was having second thoughts about springing the news of her summer adventure on Josh.

Josh took both her hands in his and stared into her eyes. "You saved my life, Wendy Valentine. I'll follow you anywhere."

Relief coursed through her as she smiled. "You pulled me out of a snowdrift and saved me from exposure, and a lot else. We're even."

"You saved me from being mauled by a mountain lion."

"You keep talking about this cat that I never saw, but okay. I saved you from a mountain lion. But we're still even."

Josh shook his head and took a step closer. "You saved me from a life of solitude. I would still be running away from the guilt of what I had done to Hank and

Vera—" he cupped her cheek with his palm "—if not for you."

Wendy, teary-eyed, kept smiling. Josh didn't often talk about the past. They had been so busy with the new job and his classes. She turned her head and kissed the palm of his hand, then wrapped her fingers around his. "For a while there I didn't think this would happen."

"It's what we in the medical community refer to as a miracle, Wendy."

"And what we in the news business refer to as a story with a happy ending." And although they had the rest of their lives together and all the time in the world, she kissed him again. After all, she did have a new motto.

* * * * *

For the first HOME TO BEAR MEADOWS *story, be sure to check out* WANTED: THE PERFECT MOM *by T. R. McClure. Available from www.Harlequin.com today!*

And look for the next heartfelt romance in the series, coming in fall 2017!

Get 2 Free Books,
Plus 2 Free Gifts—
just for trying the Reader Service!

Get 2 Free Books,
Plus <u>2</u> Free Gifts—
just for trying the Reader Service!

HOMETOWN HEARTS ♥

YES! Please send me **The Hometown Hearts Collection** in Larger Print. This collection begins with 3 FREE books and 2 FREE gifts in the first shipment. Along with my 3 free books, I'll also get the next 4 books from the Hometown Hearts Collection, in LARGER PRINT, which I may either return and owe nothing, or keep for the low price of $4.99 U.S./ $5.89 CDN each plus $2.99 for shipping and handling per shipment*. If I decide to continue, about once a month for 8 months I will get 6 or 7 more books, but will only need to pay for 4. That means 2 or 3 books in every shipment will be FREE! If I decide to keep the entire collection, I'll have paid for only 32 books because 19 books are FREE! I understand that accepting the 3 free books and gifts places me under no obligation to buy anything. I can always return a shipment and cancel at any time. My free books and gifts are mine to keep no matter what I decide.

262 HCN 3432 462 HCN 3432

Name _____ (PLEASE PRINT) _____

Address _____ Apt. # _____

City _____ State/Prov. _____ Zip/Postal Code _____

Signature (if under 18, a parent or guardian must sign)

Mail to the **Reader Service**:

IN U.S.A.: P.O. Box 1867, Buffalo, NY. 14240-1867
IN CANADA: P.O. Box 609, Fort Erie, Ontario L2A 5X3

* Terms and prices subject to change without notice. Prices do not include applicable taxes. Sales tax applicable in NY. Canadian residents will be charged applicable taxes. This offer is limited to one order per household. All orders subject to approval. Credit or debit balances in a customer's account(s) may be offset by any other outstanding balance owed by or to the customer. Please allow 4 to 6 weeks for delivery. Offer available while quantities last. Offer not available to Quebec residents.

Your Privacy—The Reader Service is committed to protecting your privacy. Our Privacy Policy is available online at www.ReaderService.com or upon request from the Reader Service.

We make a portion of our mailing list available to reputable third parties that offer products we believe may interest you. If you prefer that we not exchange your name with third parties, or if you wish to clarify or modify your communication preferences, please visit us at www.ReaderService.com/consumerschoice or write to us at Reader Service Preference Service, P.O. Box 9062, Buffalo, NY. 14240-9062. Include your complete name and address.

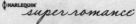

Get 2 Free Books,
Plus 2 Free Gifts—
just for trying the
Reader Service!

Love Inspired® HISTORICAL

LIHI17R